SILLY LILLY

IN WHAT WILL I BE TODAY?

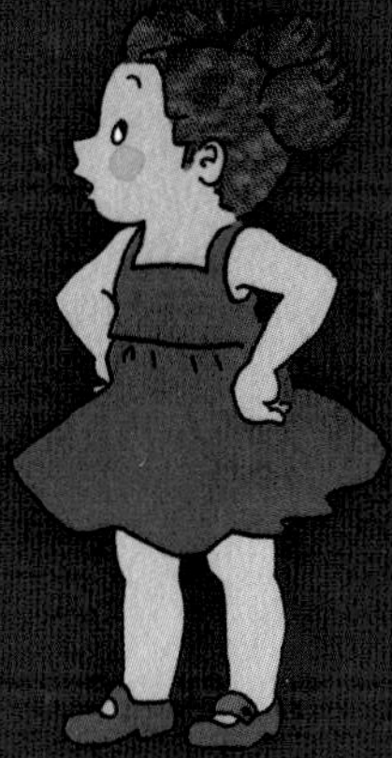

Agnès Rosenstiehl

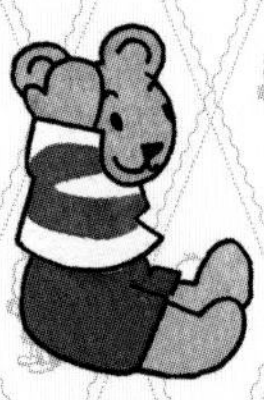

SILLY LILLY

IN WHAT WILL I BE TODAY?

What about *you*, Teddy?

A TOON BOOK BY

Agnès Rosenstiehl

TOON BOOKS IS A DIVISION OF **RAW** JUNIOR, LLC, NEW YORK

Visit us at www.abdopublishing.com
Reinforced library bound editions published in 2014 by Spotlight, a division of the ABDO Group, PO Box 398166, Minneapolis, MN 55439. Spotlight produces high-quality reinforced library bound editions for schools and libraries.
Reprinted by agreement with Raw Junior, LLC.

Printed in the United States of America, North Mankato, Minnesota.
042013
092013
This book contains at least 10% recycled material.

For Ella Choudhury

Editorial Director: Francoise Mouly, Book Design: Francoise Mouly & Jonathan Bennett.
Agnès Rosenstiehl's artwork was drawn in india ink & watercolor.

Library of Congress Cataloging-in-Publication Data
This book was previously cataloged with the following information:

Rosenstiehl, Agnès.
Silly Lilly in what will I be today? / by Agnès Rosenstiehl.
p. cm. -- (TOON Books)
Summary: Silly Lilly tries out a new job every day of the week, from acrobat to vampire.
[1. Occupations--Fiction. 2. Cartoons and comics.] I. Title.
PZ7.R71942Sil 2010
[E]--dc22

2010005308

ISBN 978-1-61479-156-0 (reinforced library bound edition)

Spotlight

All Spotlight books are reinforced library bindings
and manufactured in the United States of America.

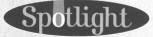

7 DAYS OF THE WEEK

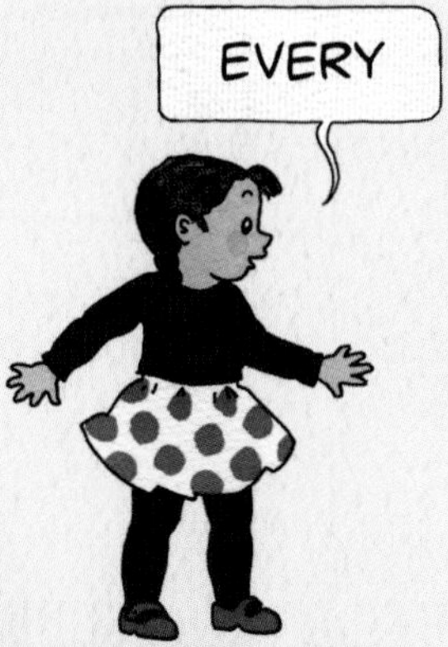
EVERY

MONDAY

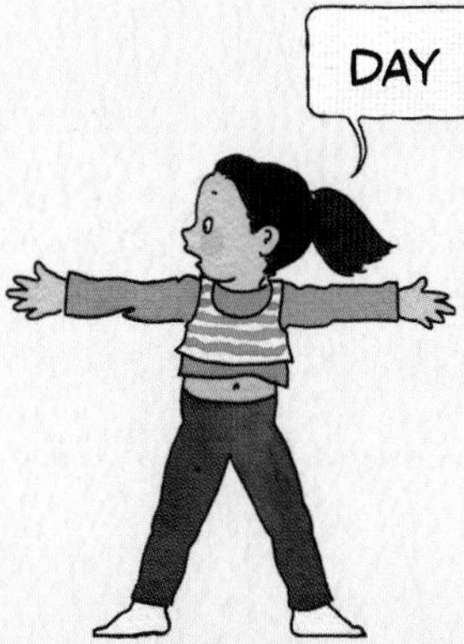
DAY

TUESDAY

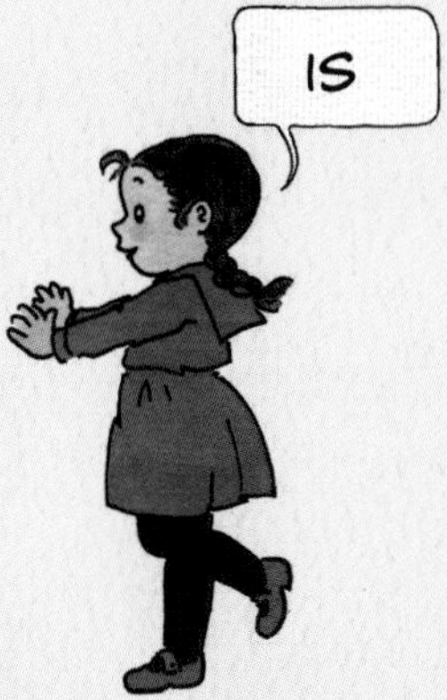
IS

WEDNESDAY

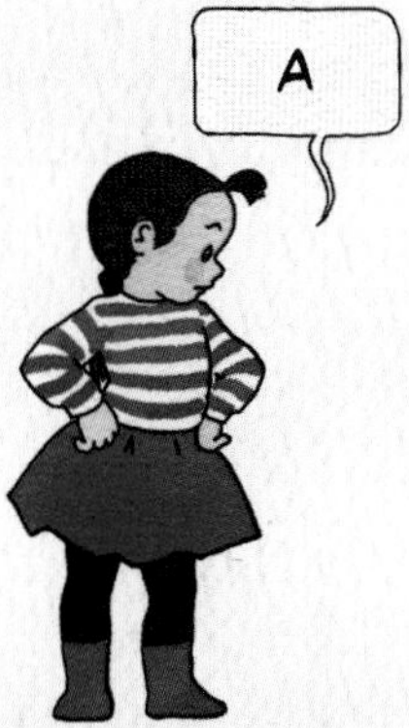
A

THURSDAY

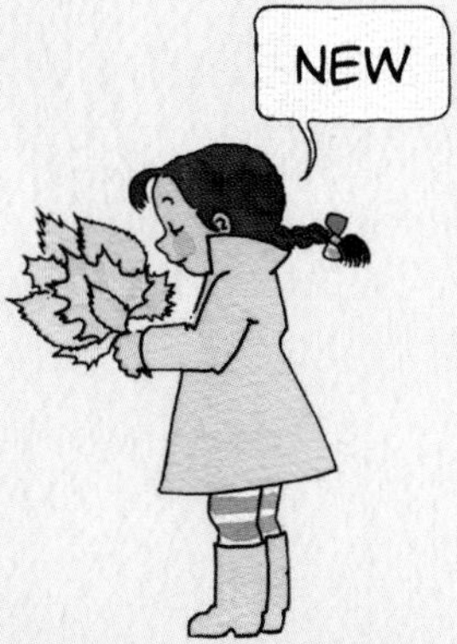
NEW

FRIDAY

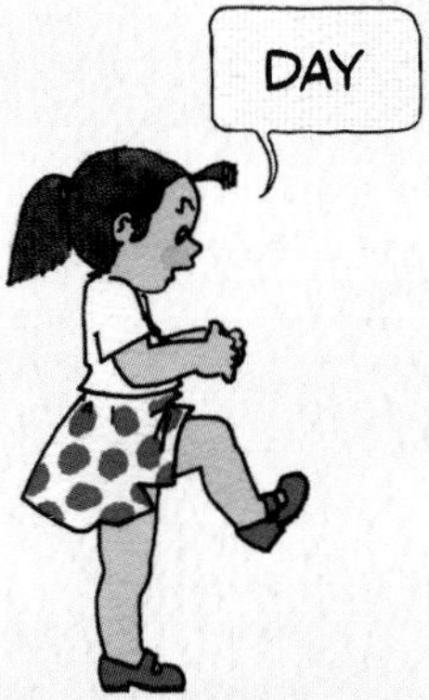
DAY

SATURDAY

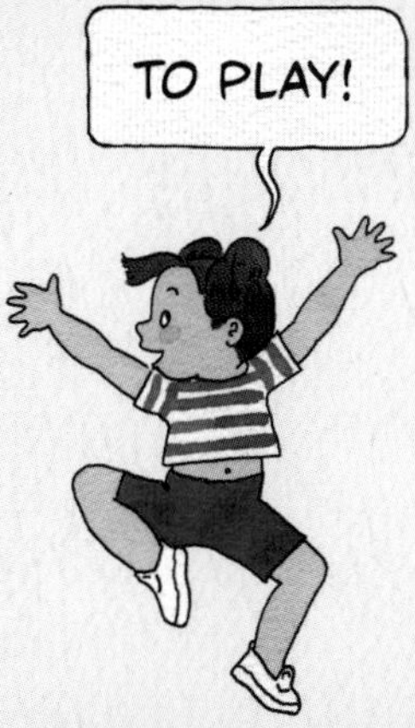
TO PLAY!

SUNDAY

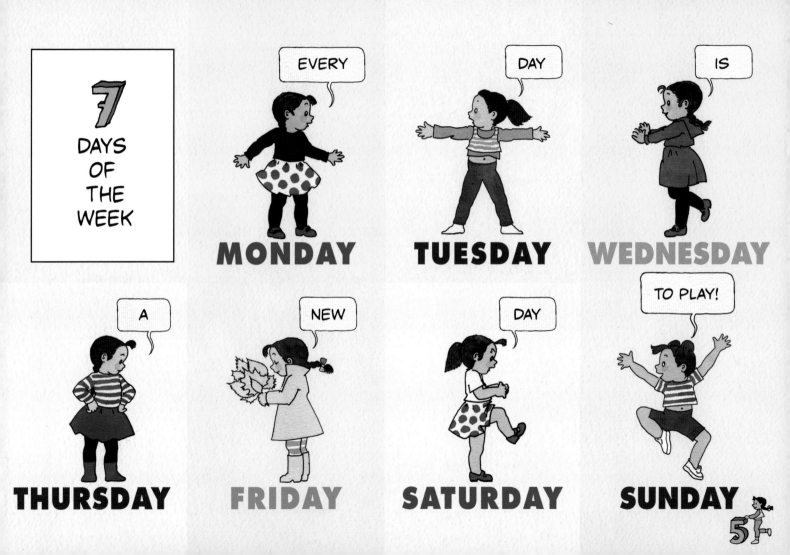

SO, ON MONDAY

SILLY LILLY

IS A COOK

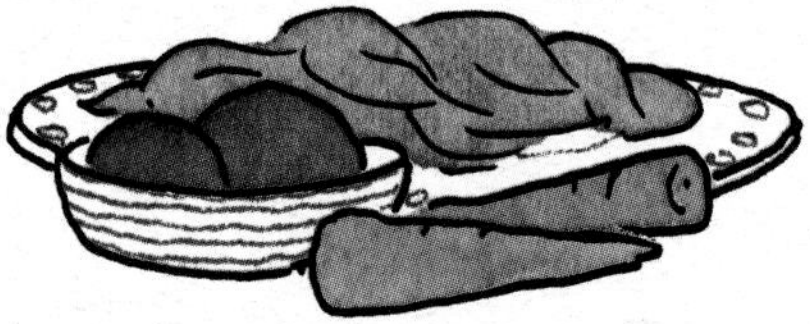

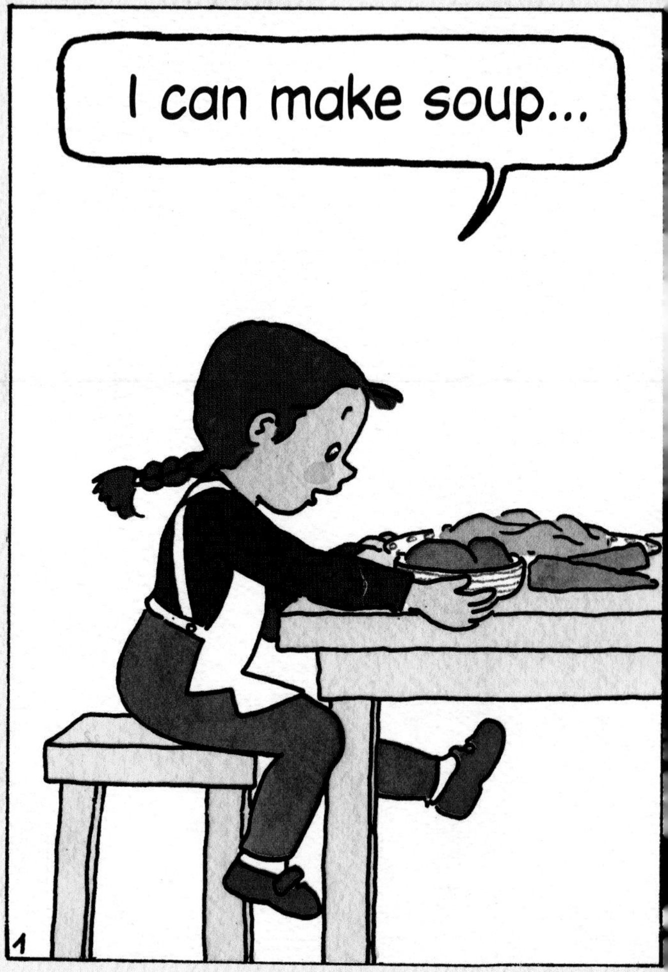
I can make soup...
1

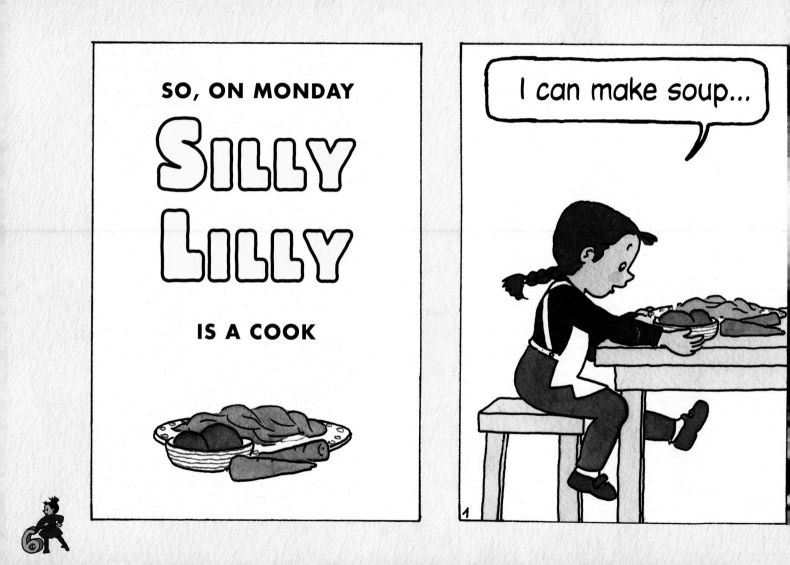

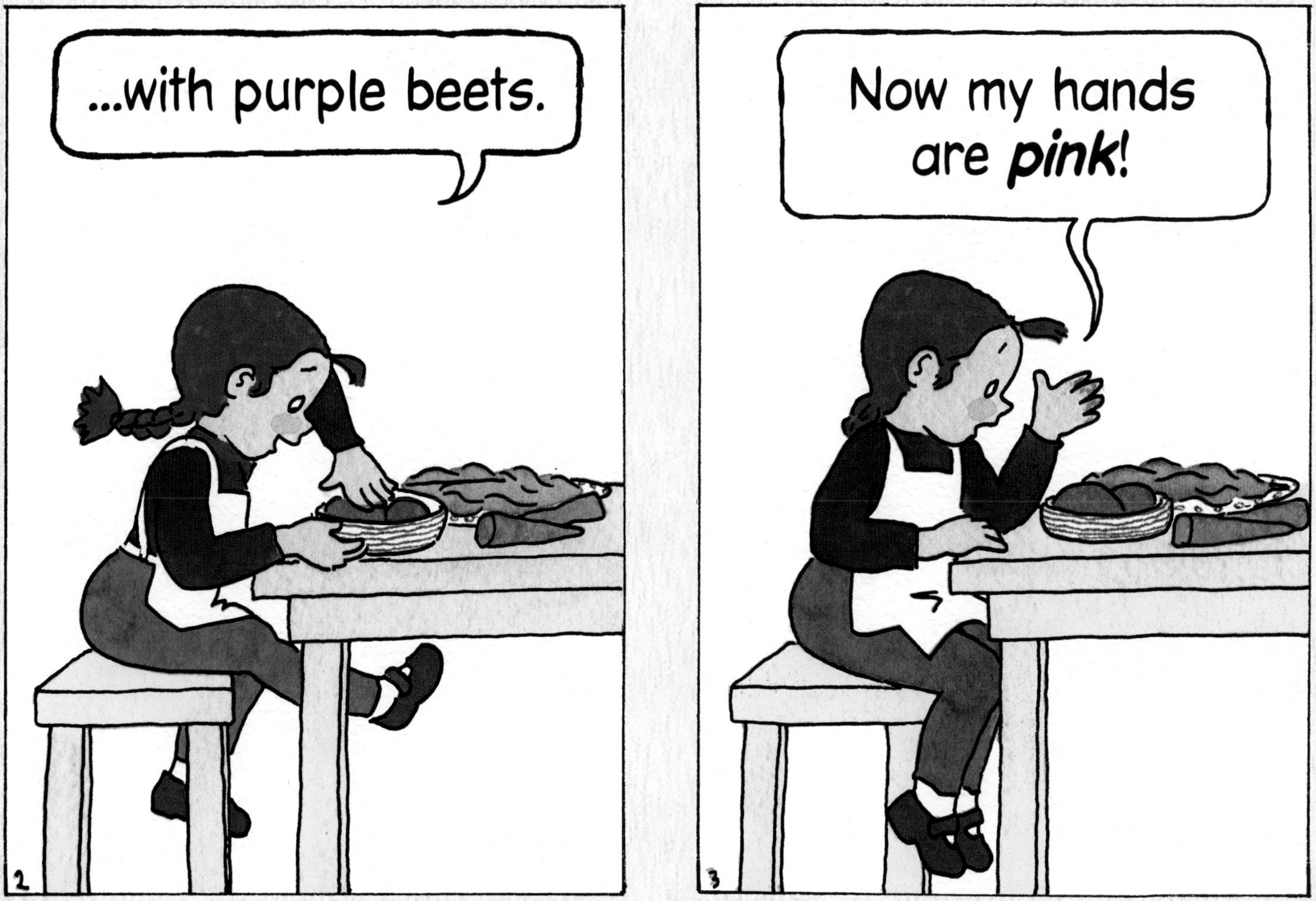
...with purple beets.
Now my hands are ***pink***!

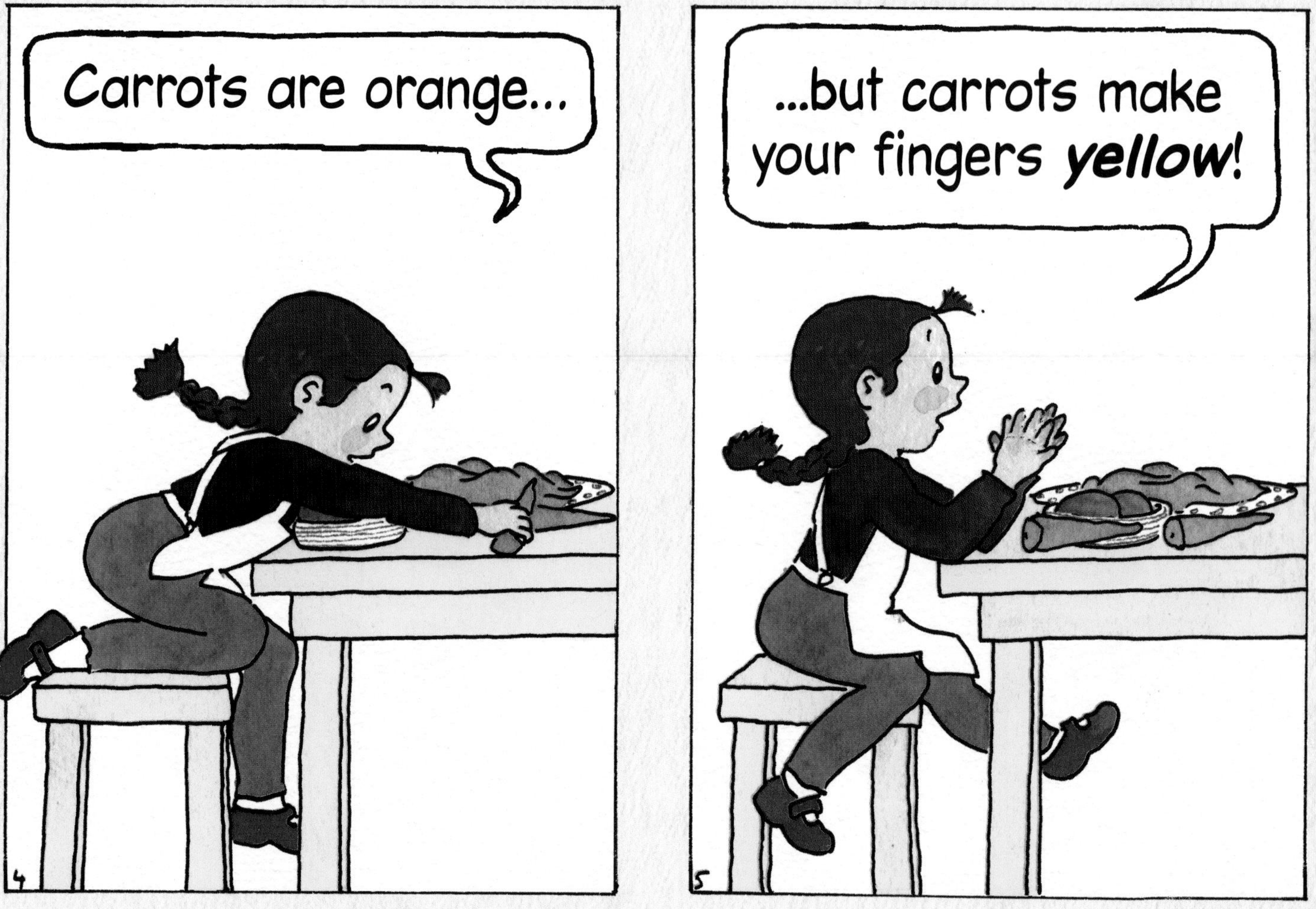
Carrots are orange...
...but carrots make your fingers ***yellow***!

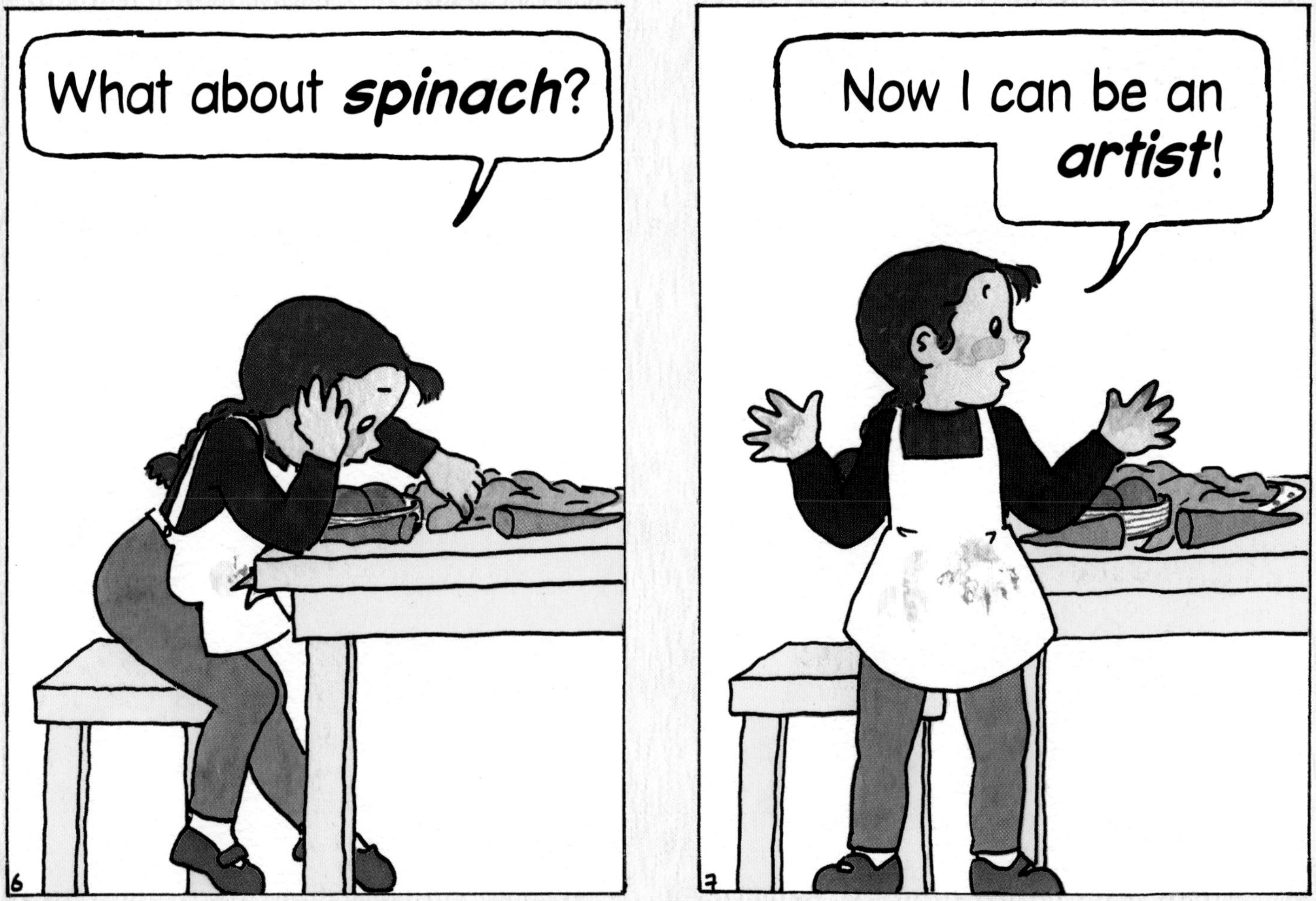
What about ***spinach***?
6
Now I can be an ***artist***!
7

SO, ON TUESDAY

SILLY LILLY

IS A CITY PLANNER

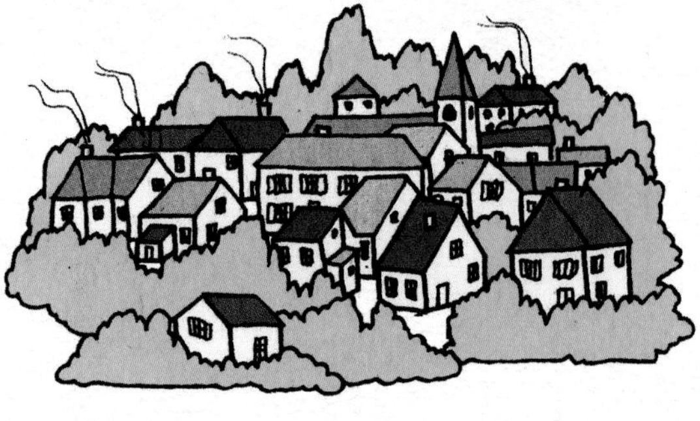

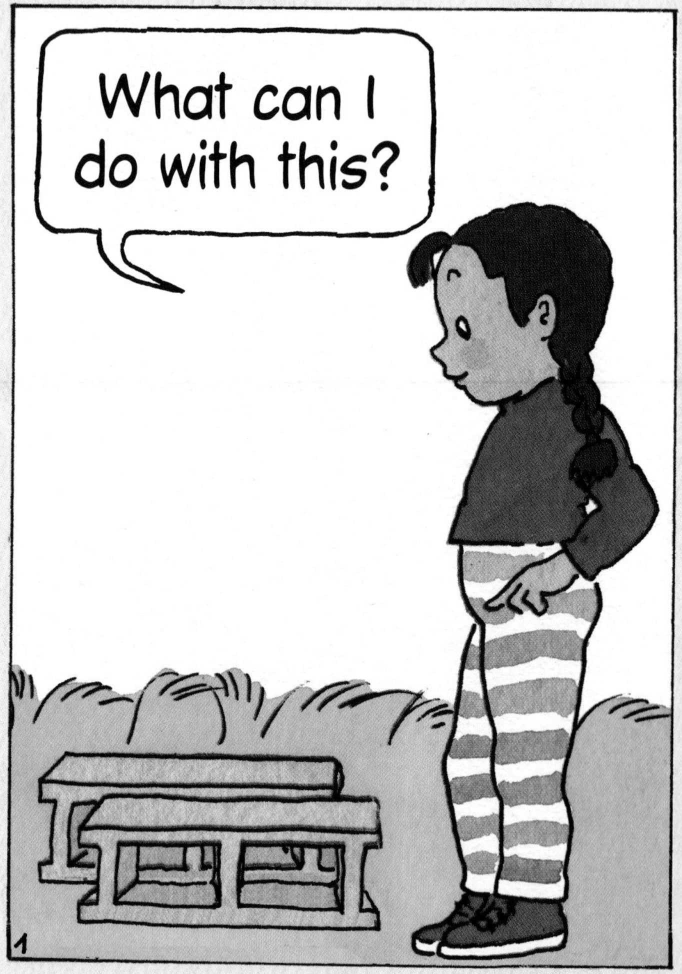
What can I do with this?
1

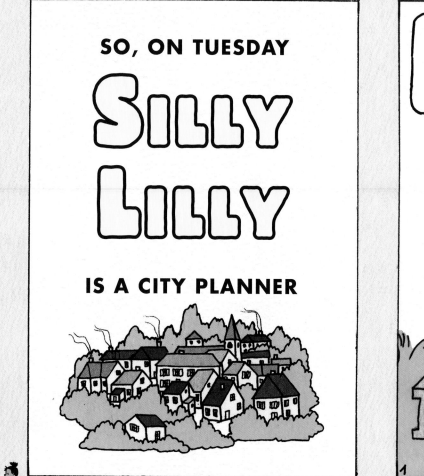

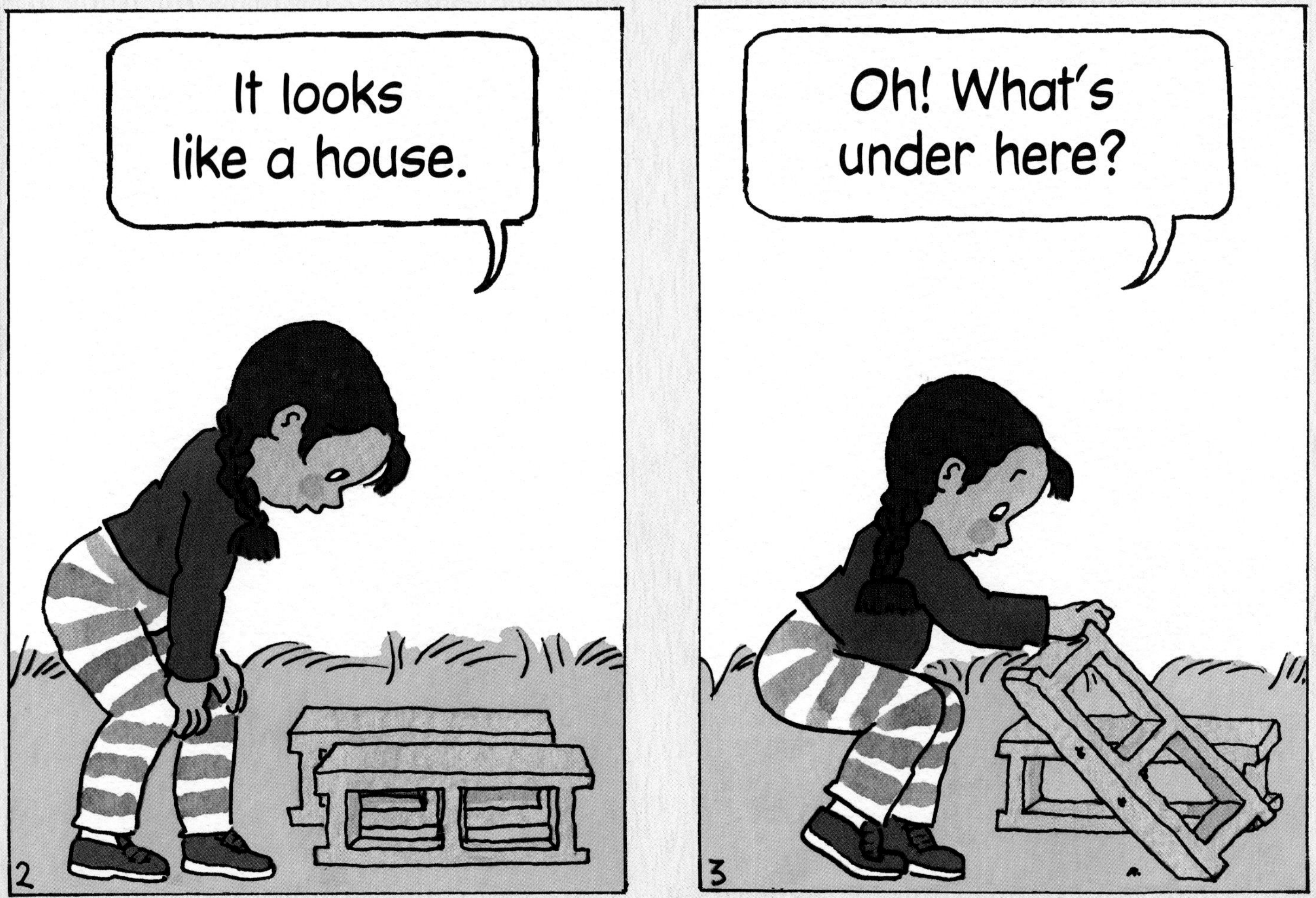
It looks like a house.
2
Oh! What's under here?
3

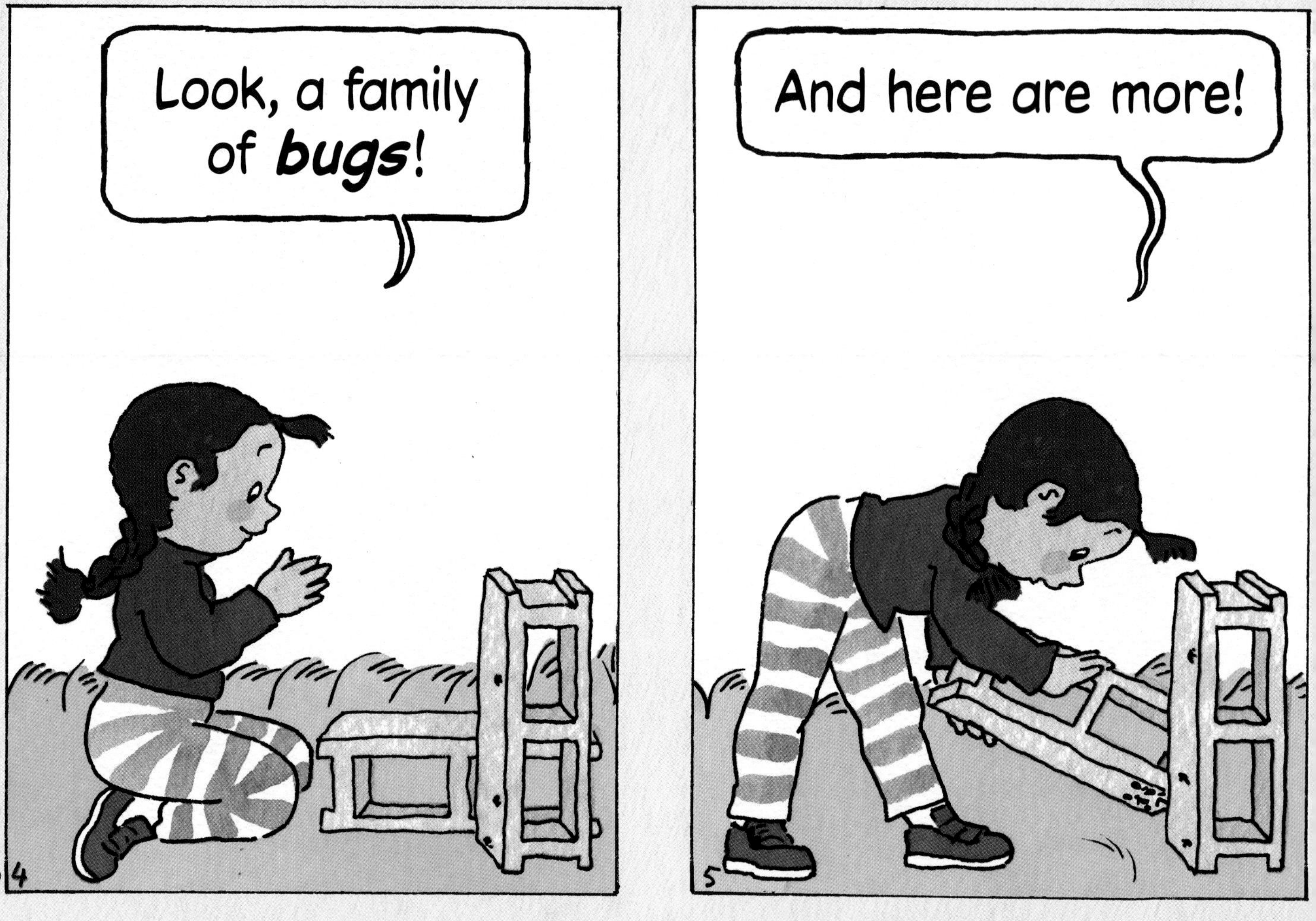
Look, a family of **bugs**!
4
And here are more!
5

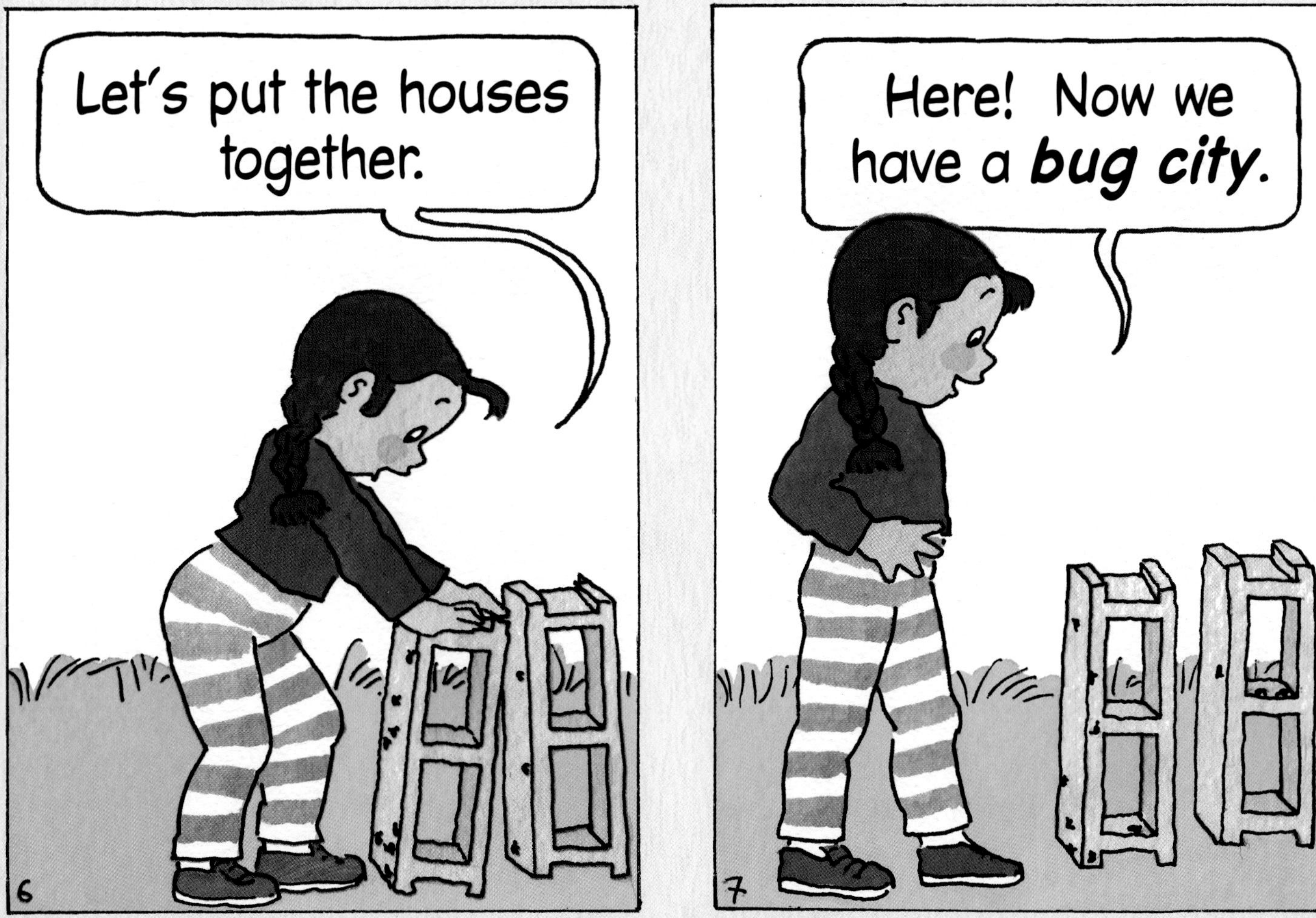
Let's put the houses together.
6
Here! Now we have a ***bug city***.
7

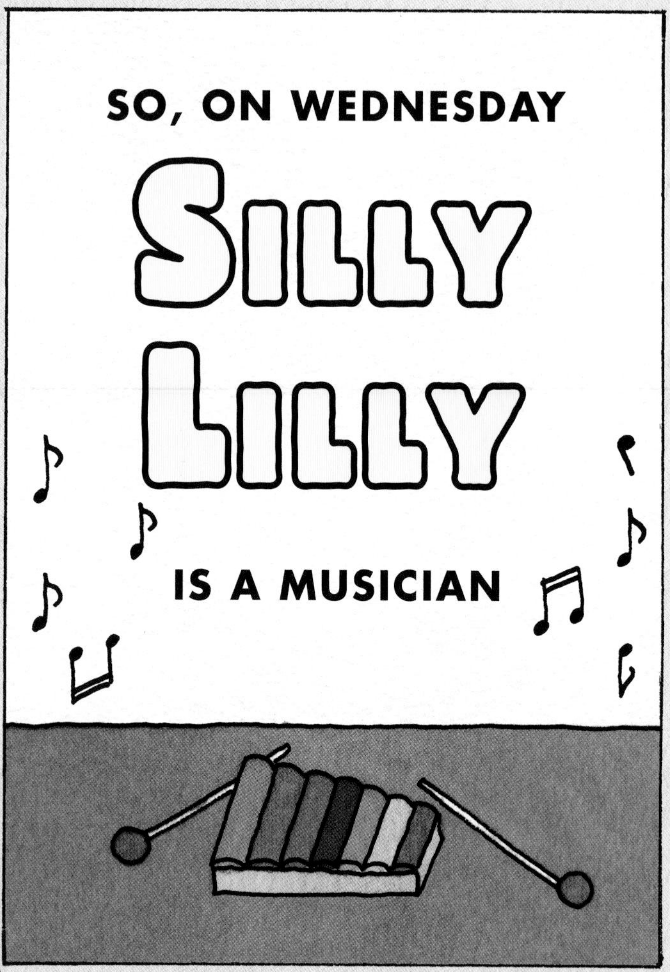
SO, ON WEDNESDAY
SILLY LILLY
IS A MUSICIAN

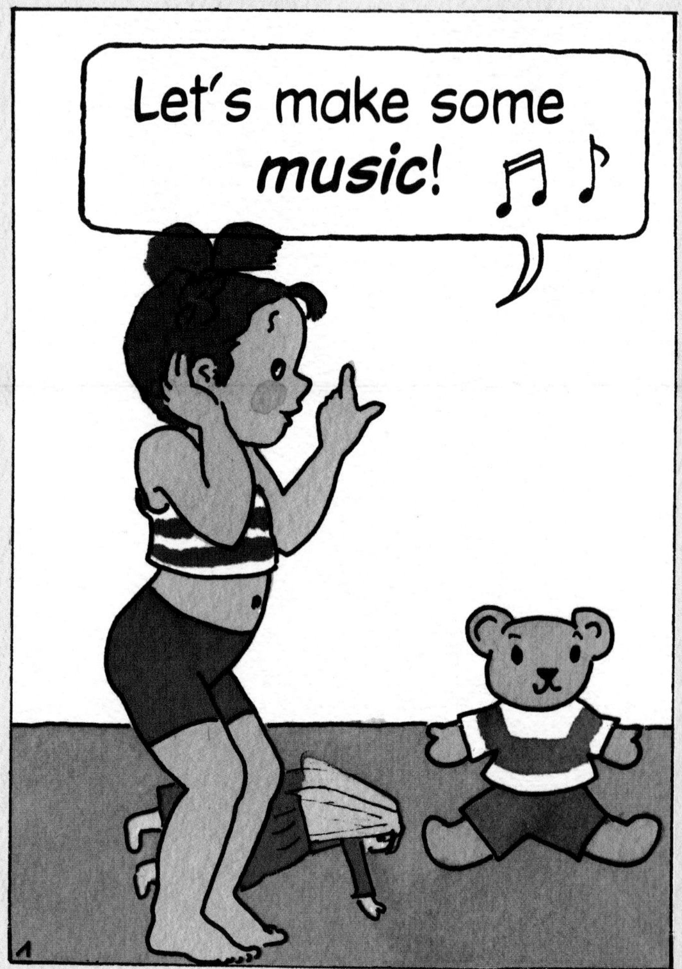
Let's make some *music*!

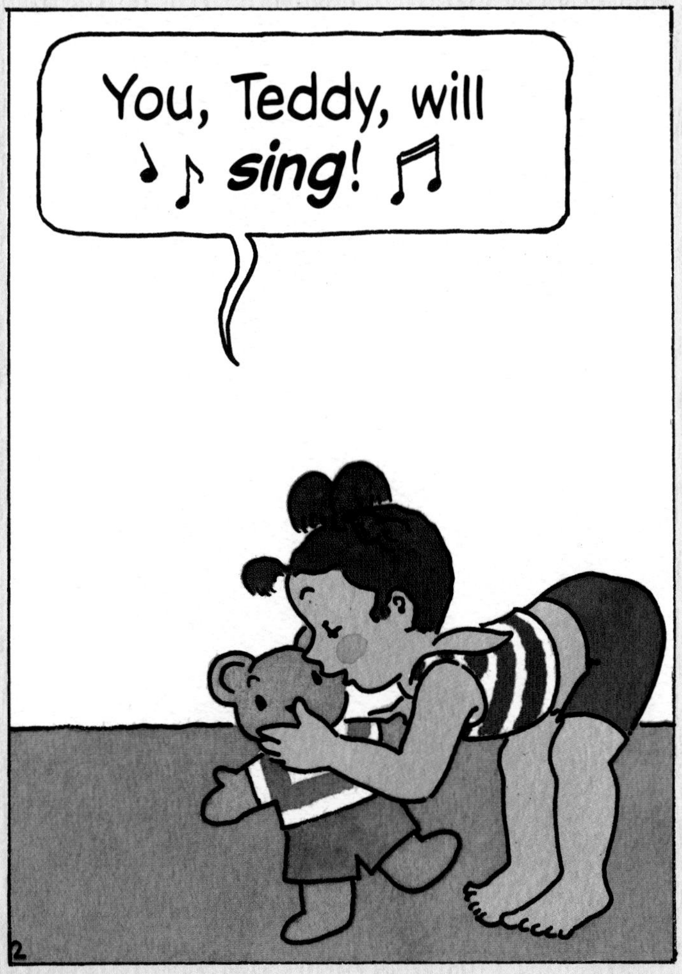
You, Teddy, will ♪ ♪ *sing*! ♫

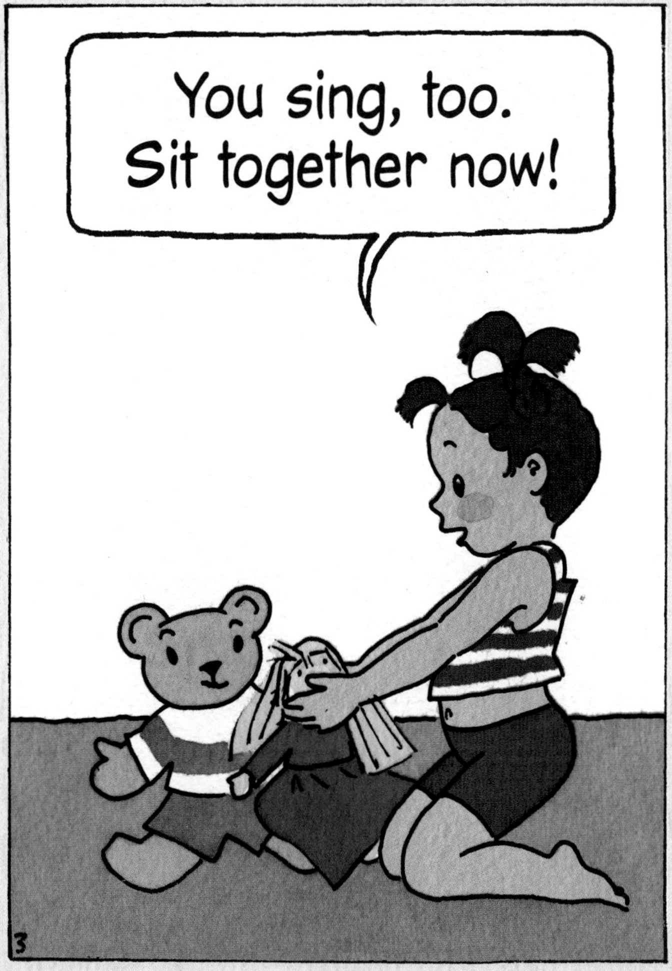
You sing, too. Sit together now!

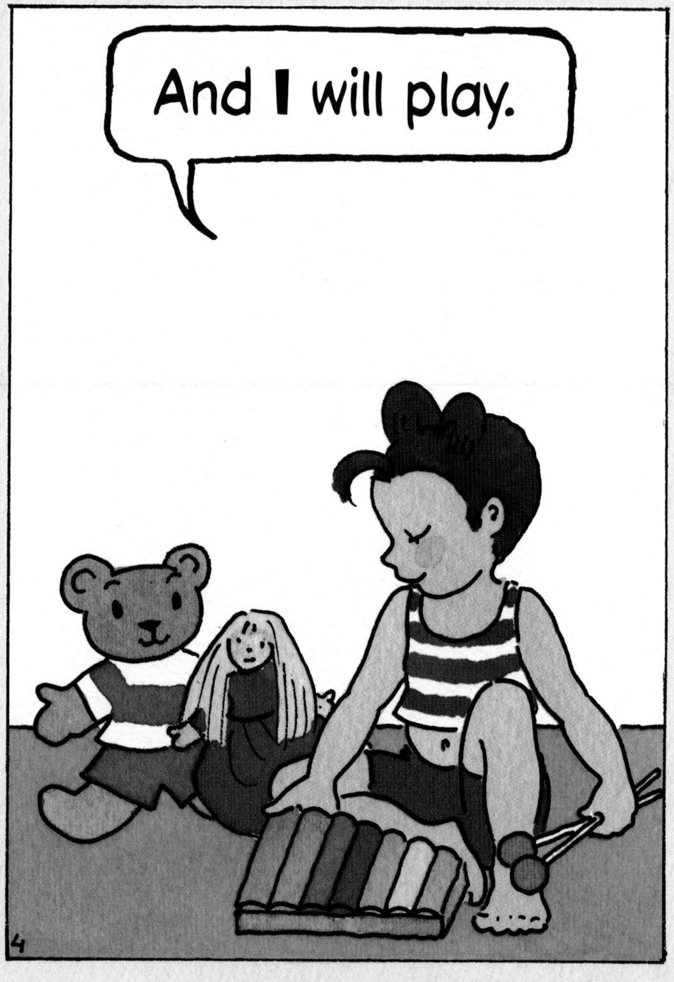
And I will play.
4

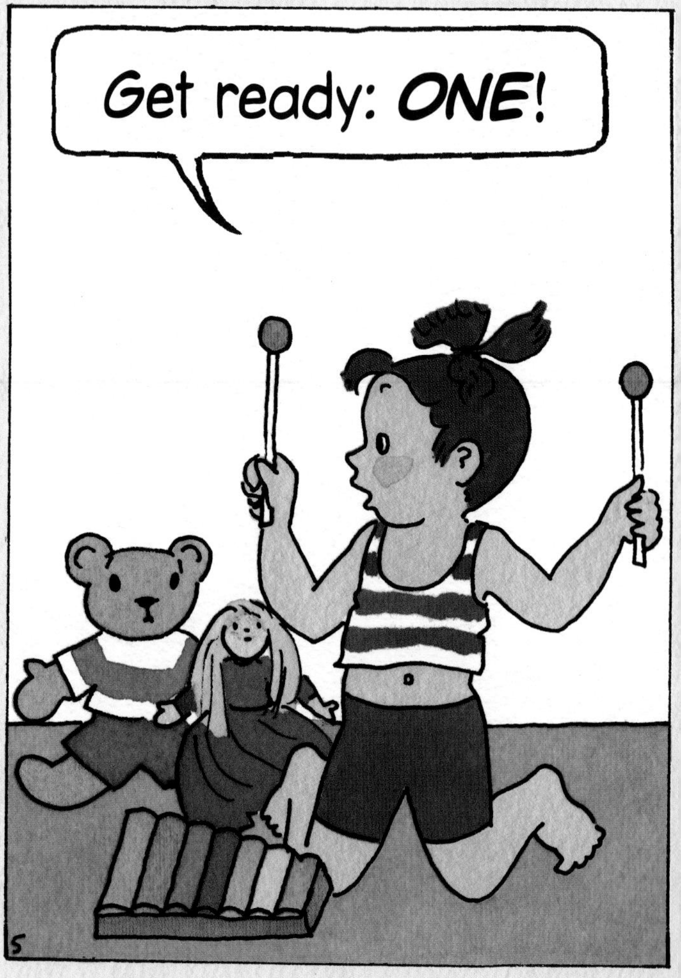
Get ready: ***ONE***!
5

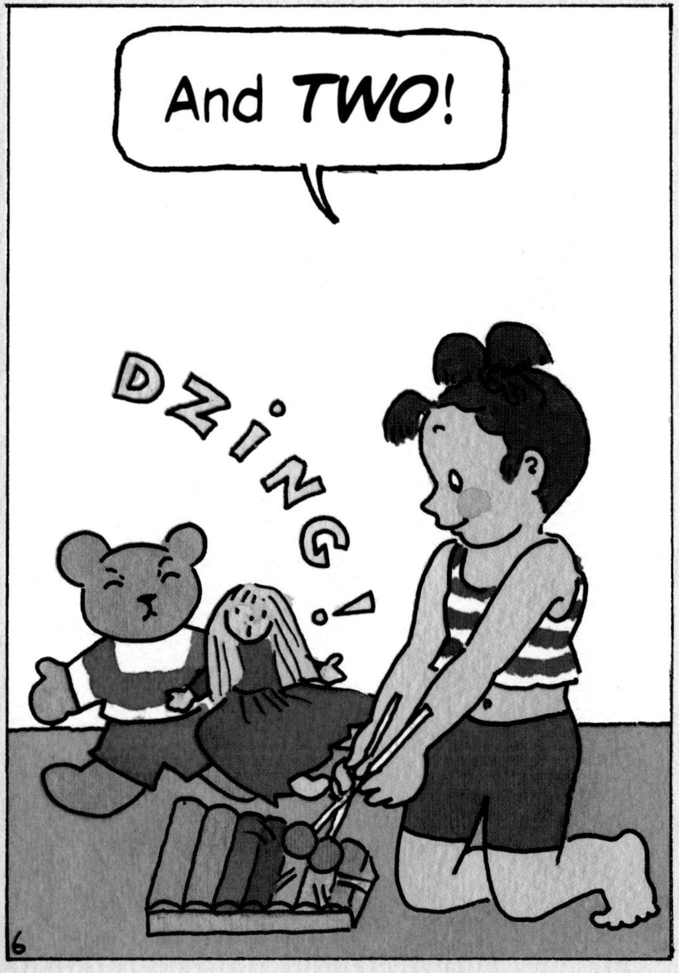
And TWO!
DZING!
6

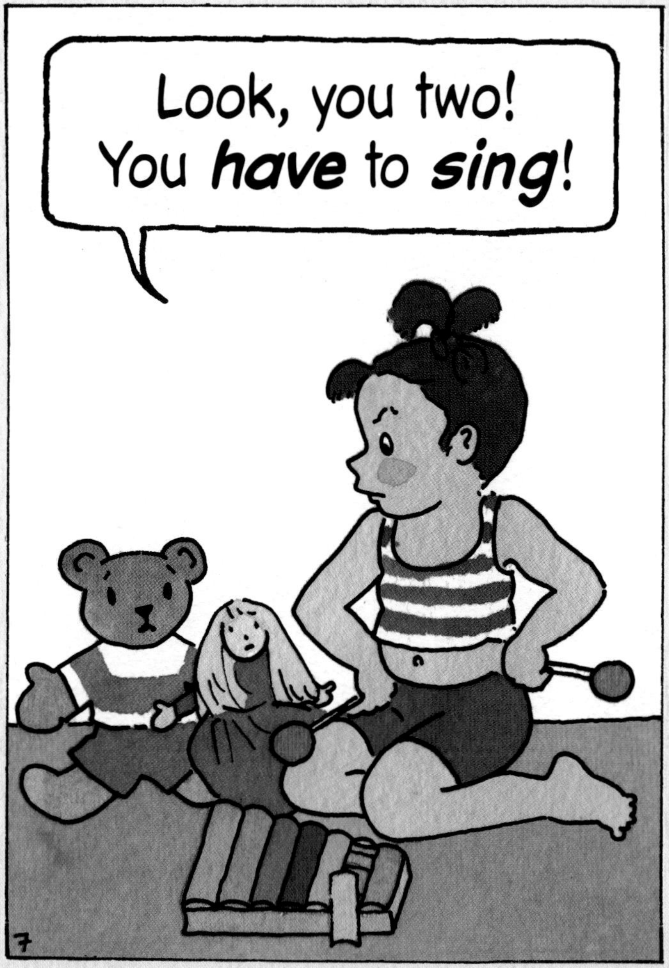
Look, you two!
You have to sing!
7

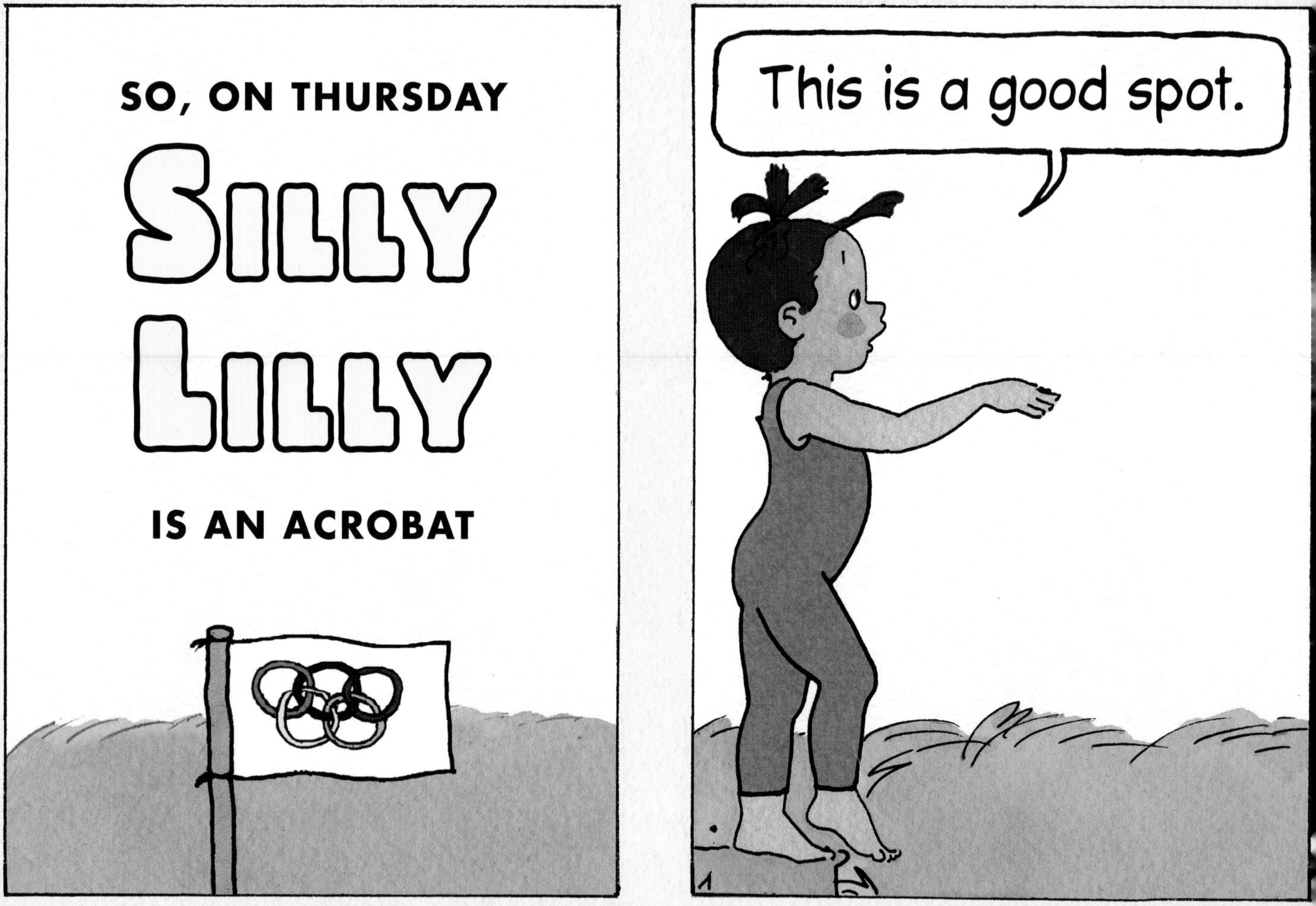
SO, ON THURSDAY
SILLY LILLY
IS AN ACROBAT
This is a good spot.

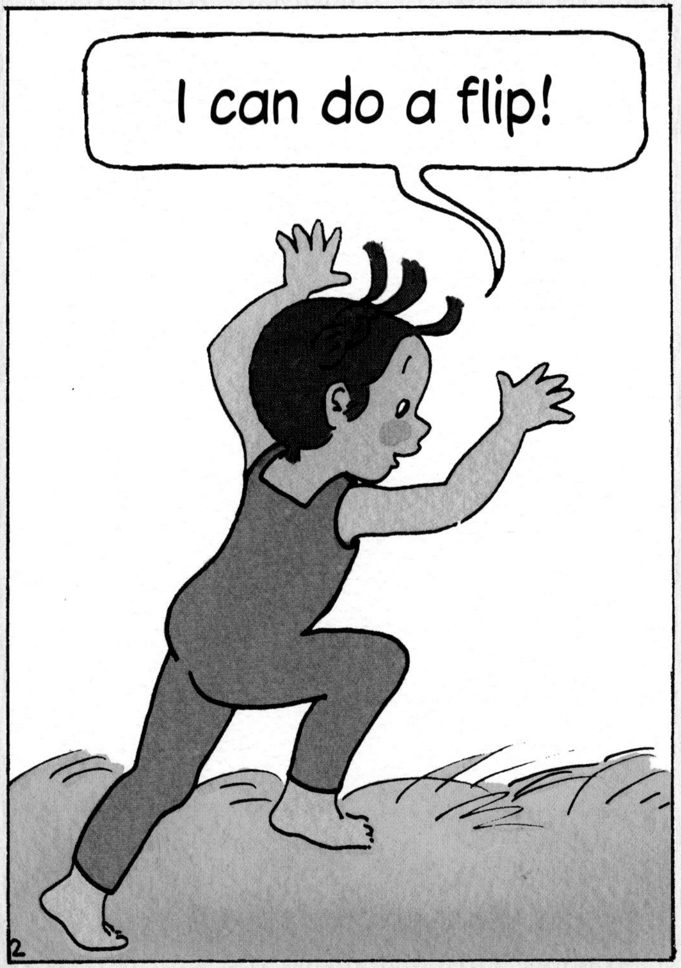
I can do a flip!

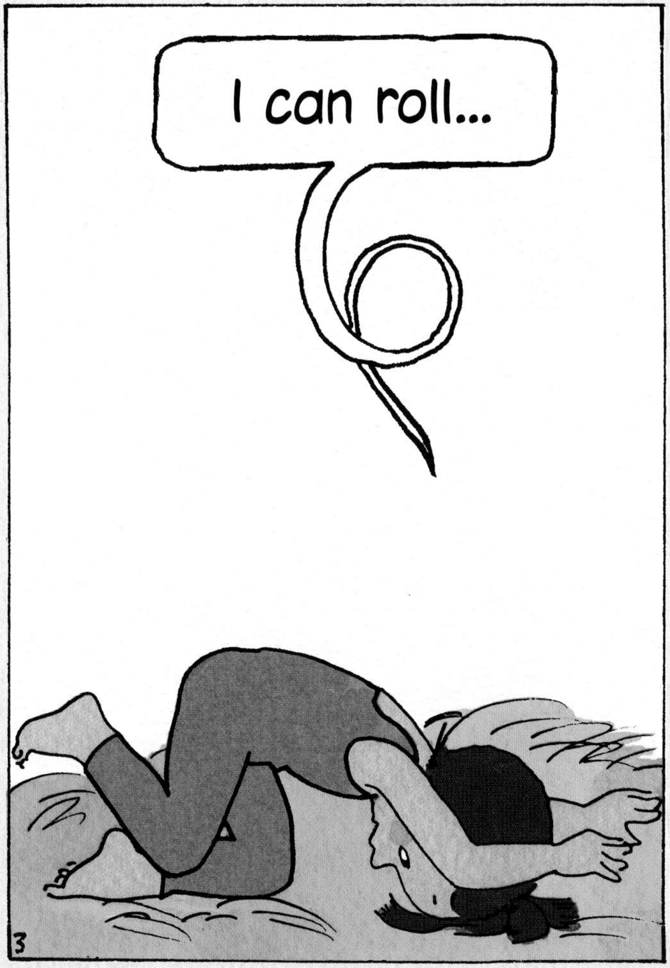
I can roll...

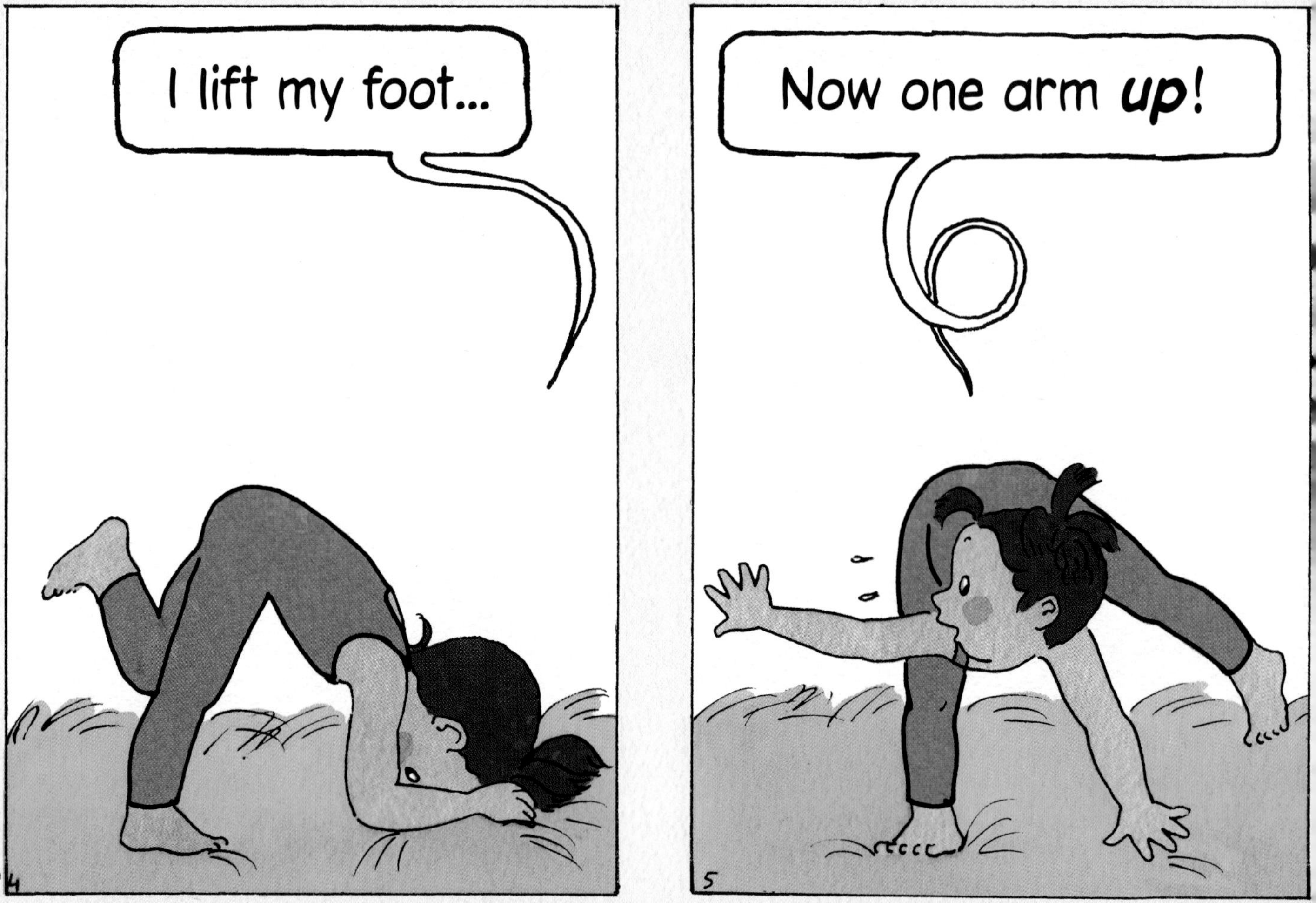
I lift my foot...
Now one arm ***up***!

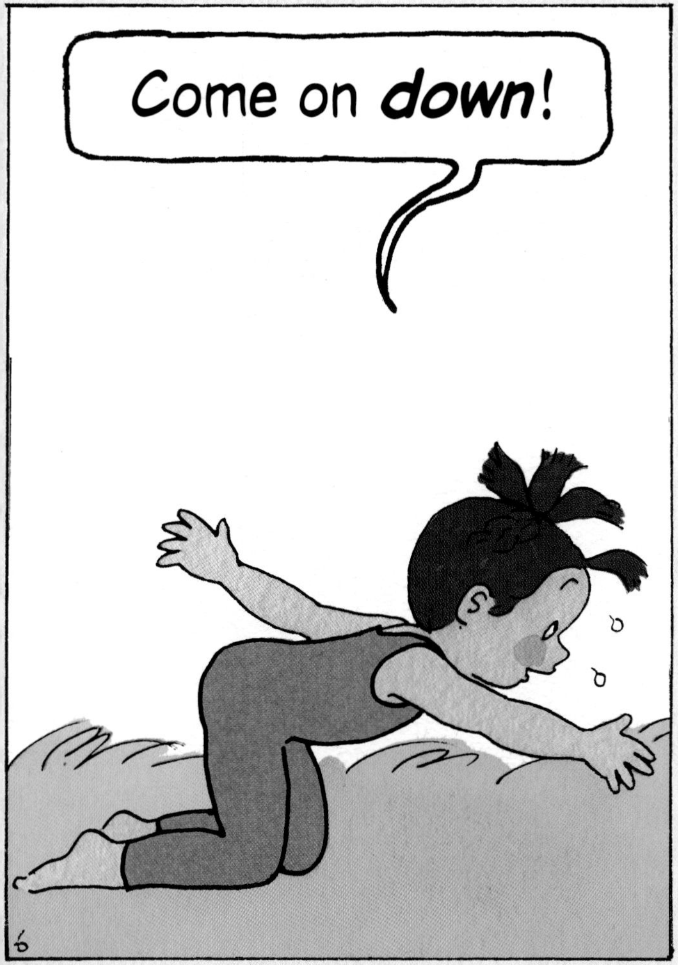
Come on **down**!

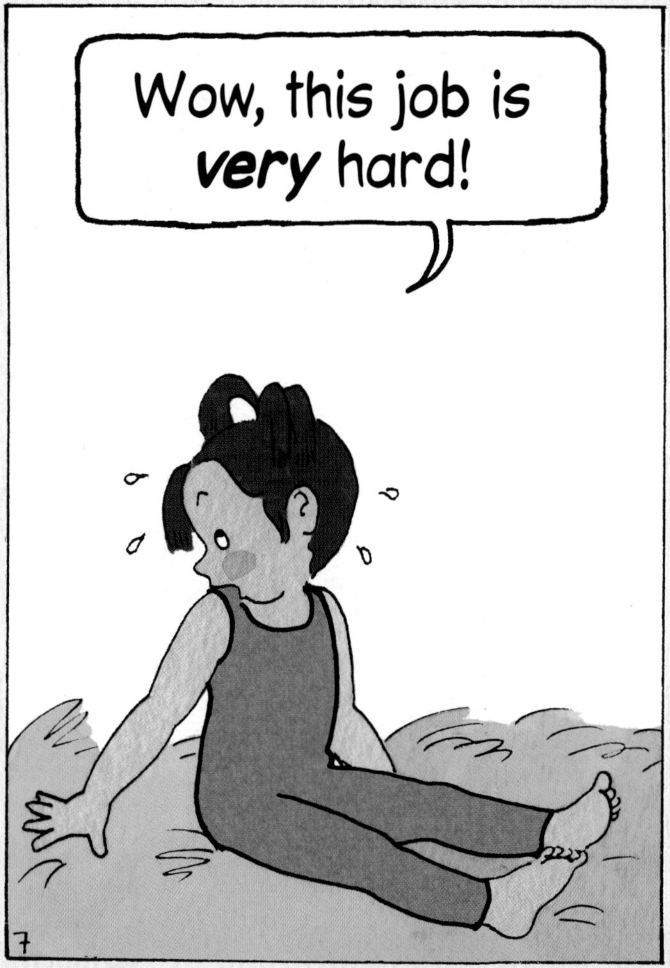
Wow, this job is **very** hard!

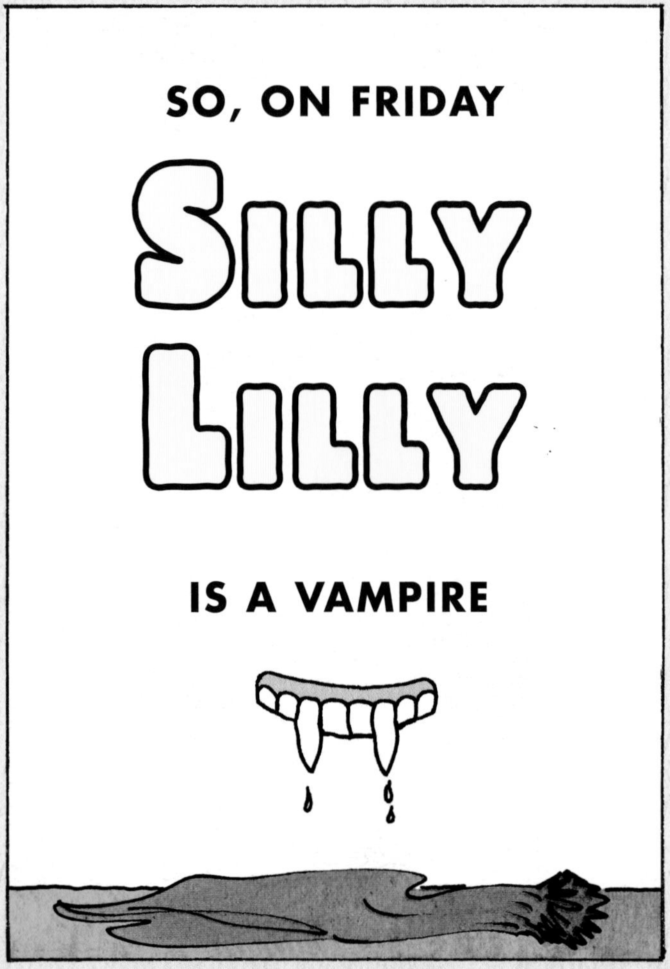
SO, ON FRIDAY
SILLY LILLY
IS A VAMPIRE

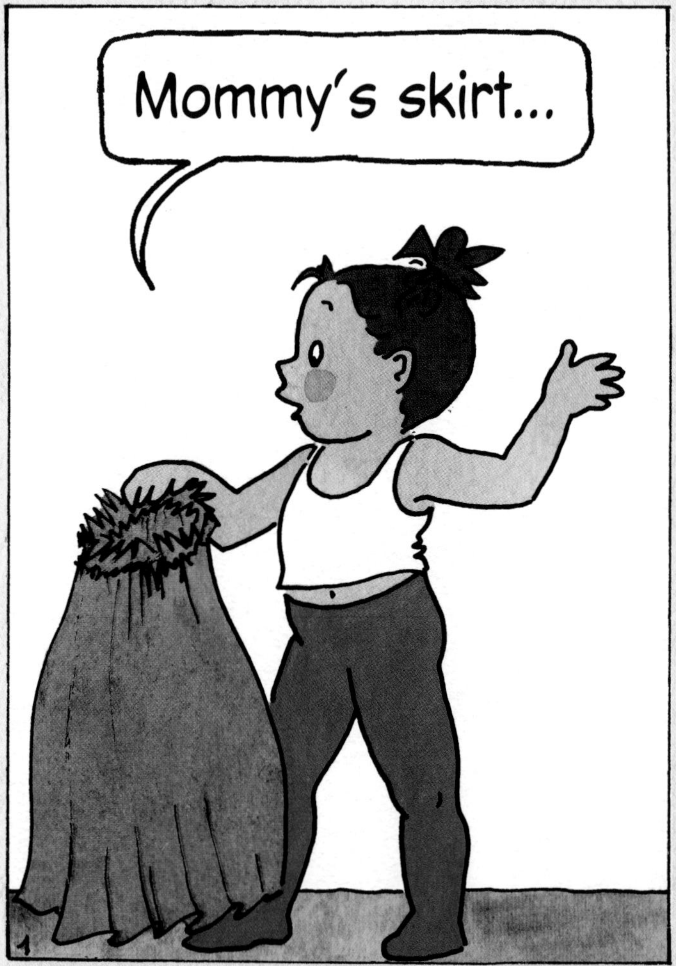
Mommy's skirt...

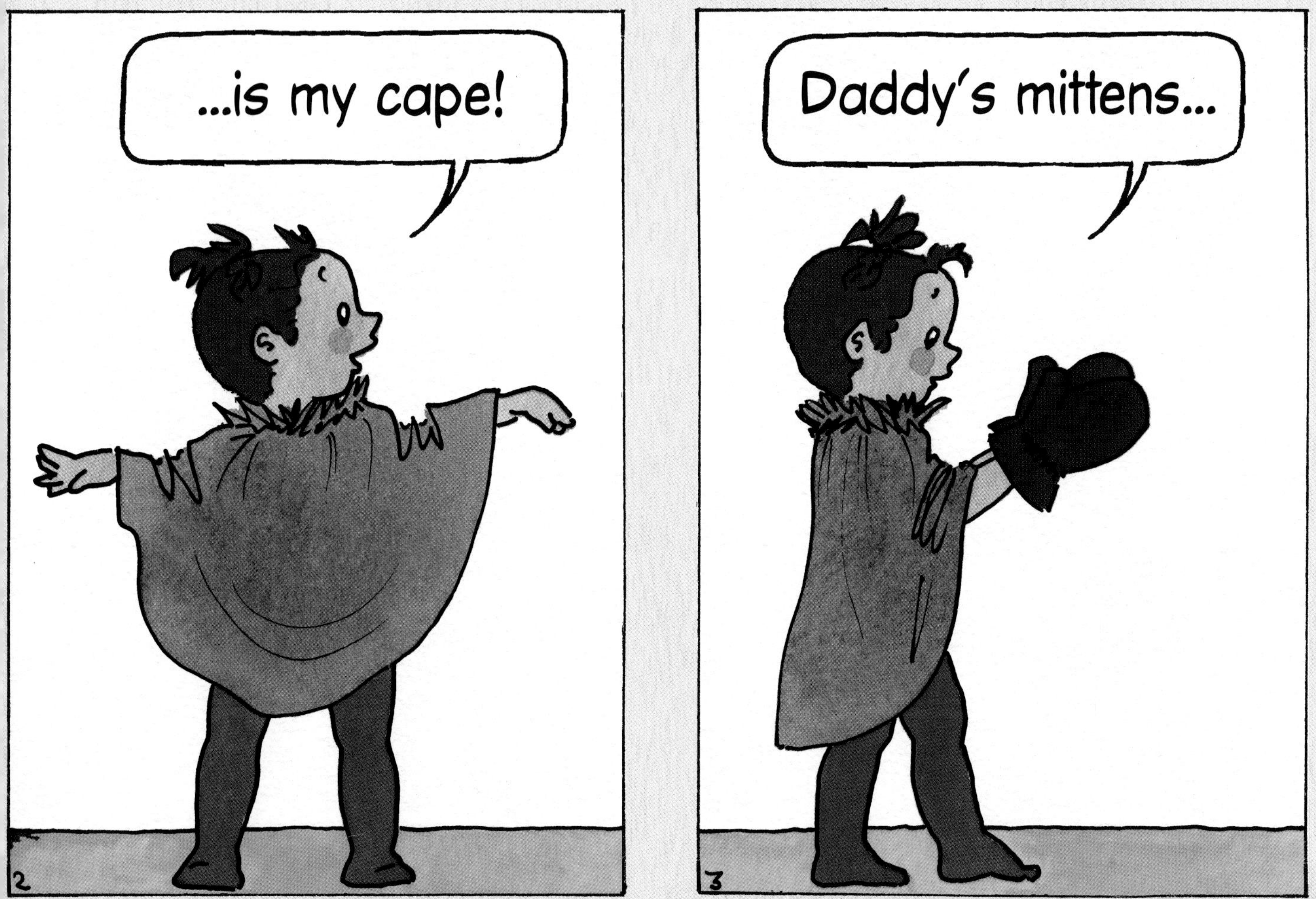
...is my cape!
Daddy's mittens...

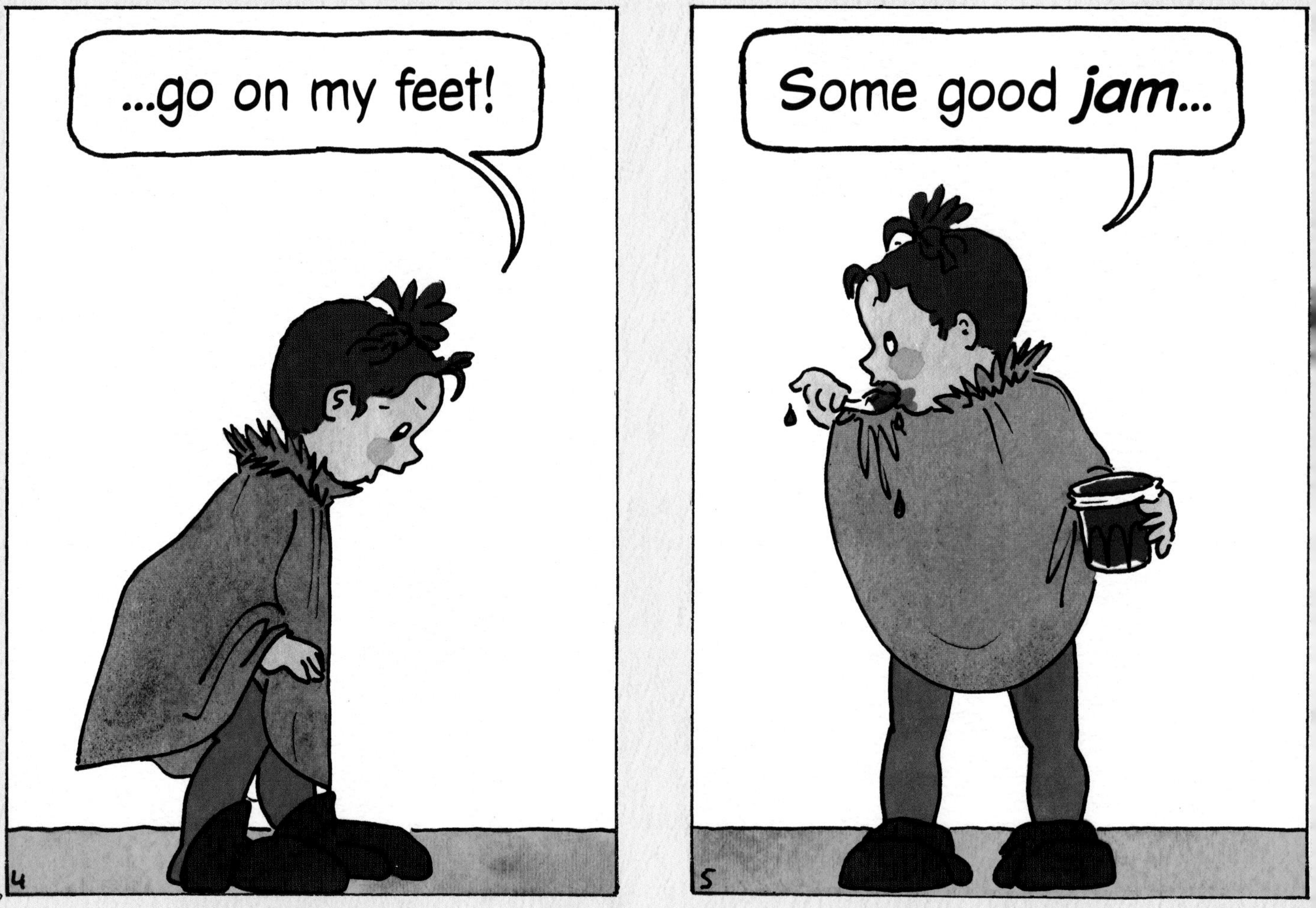
...go on my feet!
4
Some good jam...
5

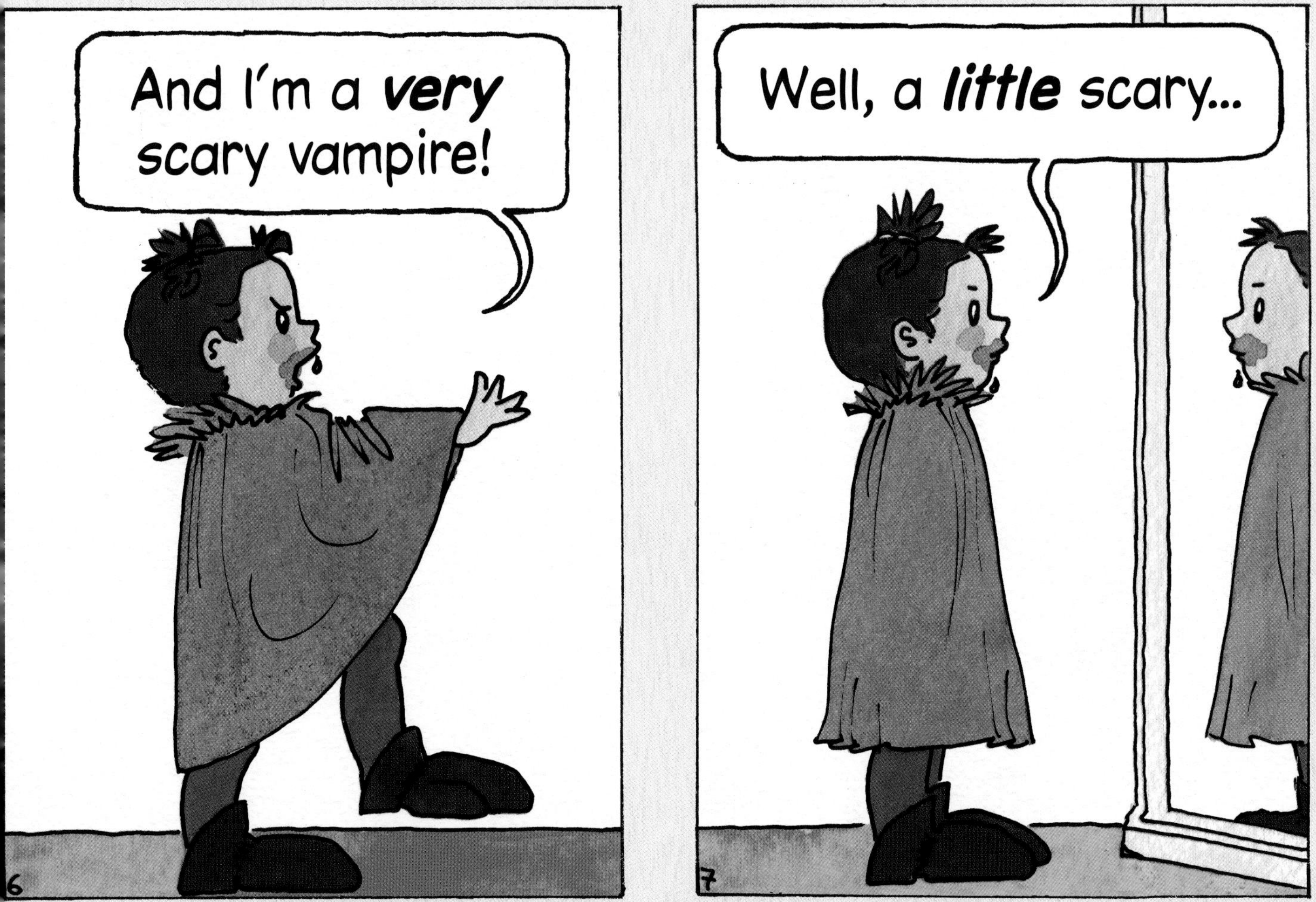
And I'm a *very* scary vampire!
Well, a *little* scary...

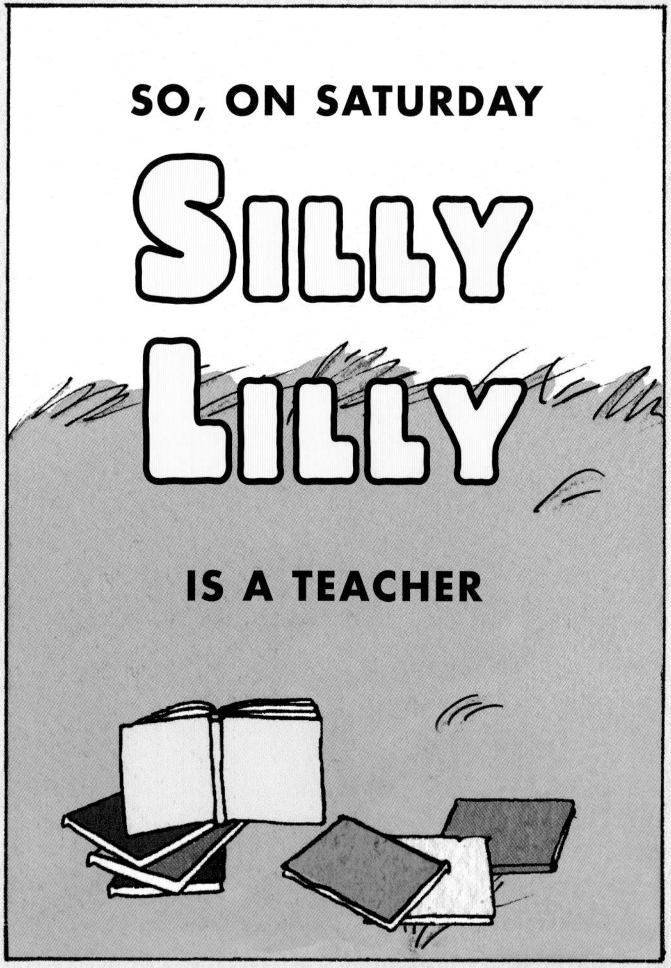
SO, ON SATURDAY
SILLY LILLY
IS A TEACHER

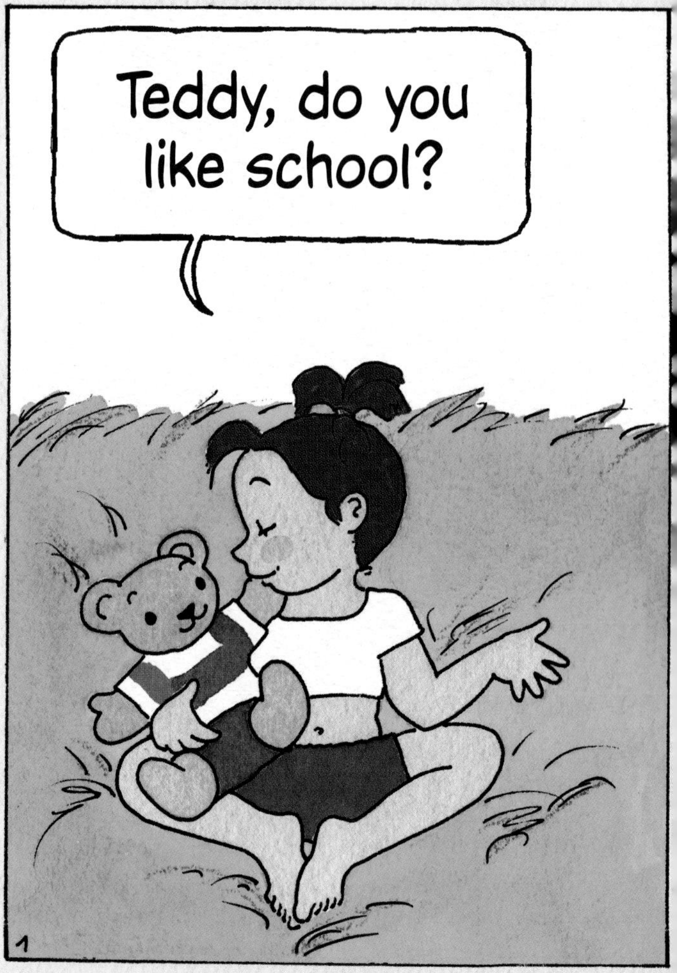
Teddy, do you like school?
1

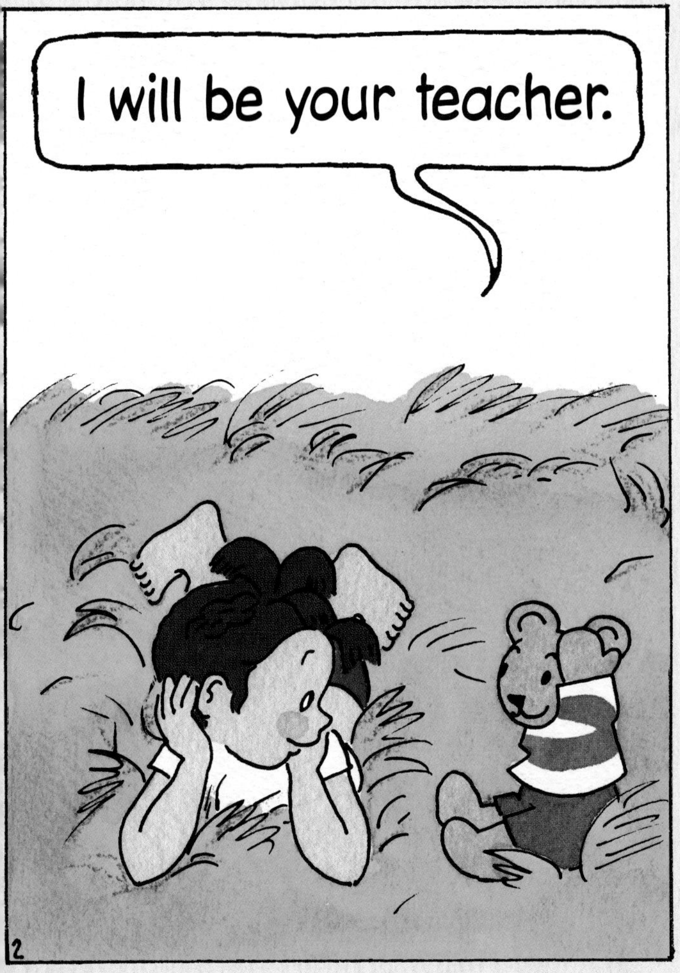
I will be your teacher.

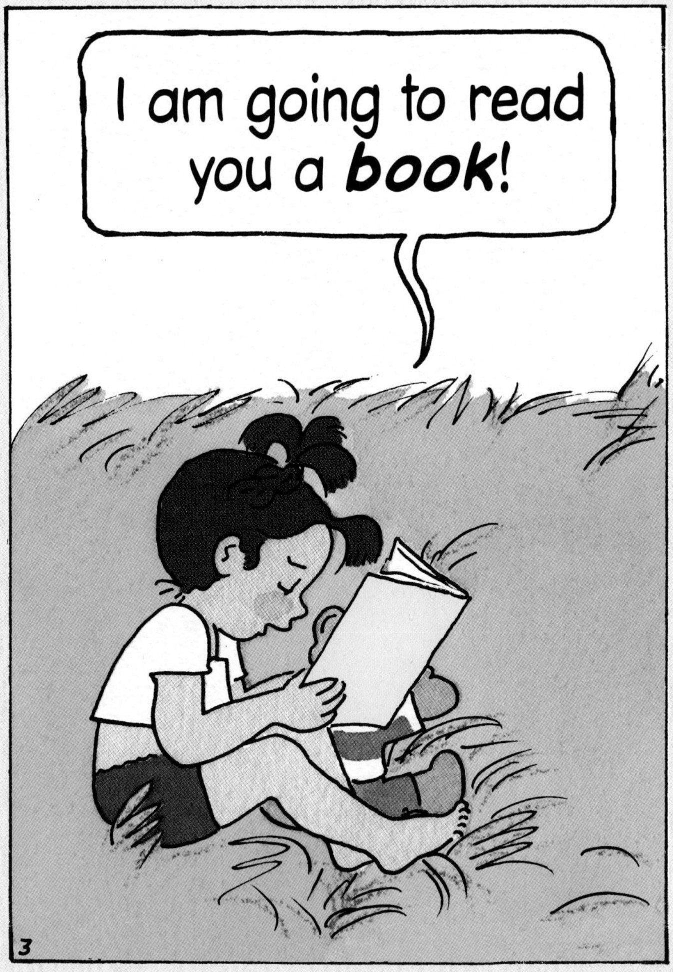
I am going to read you a **book**!

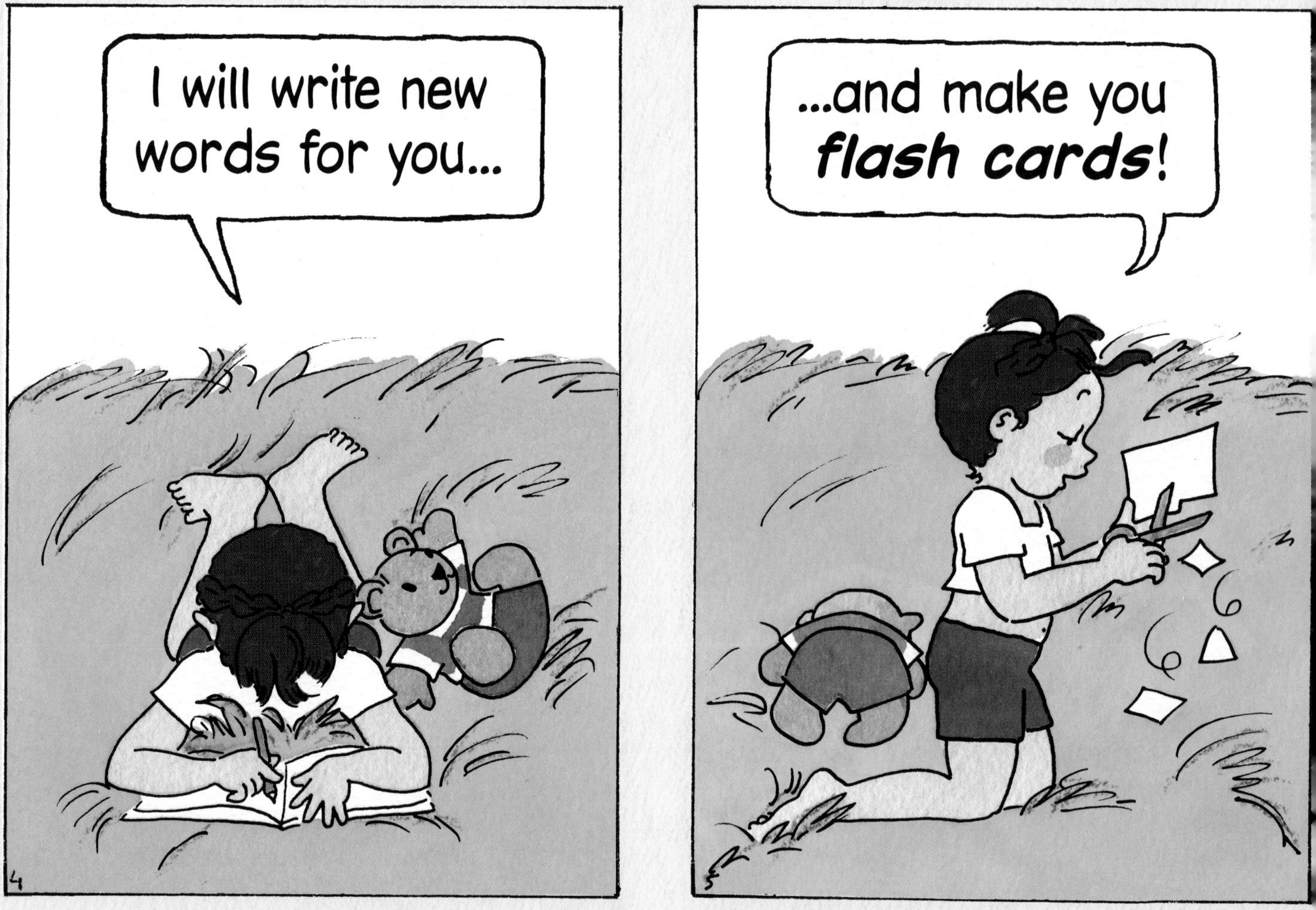
I will write new words for you...
...and make you ***flash cards***!

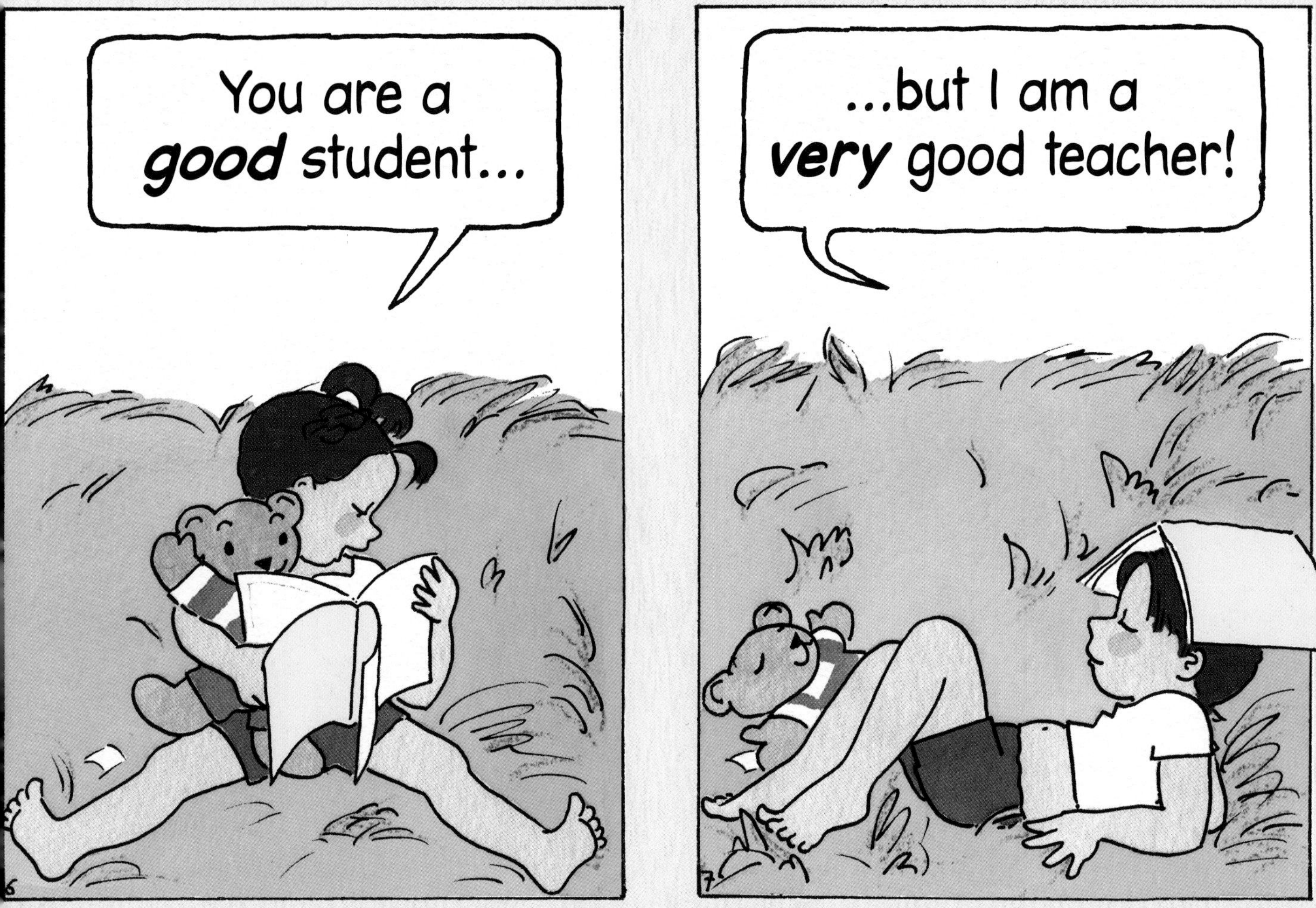
You are a **good** student...
...but I am a **very** good teacher!

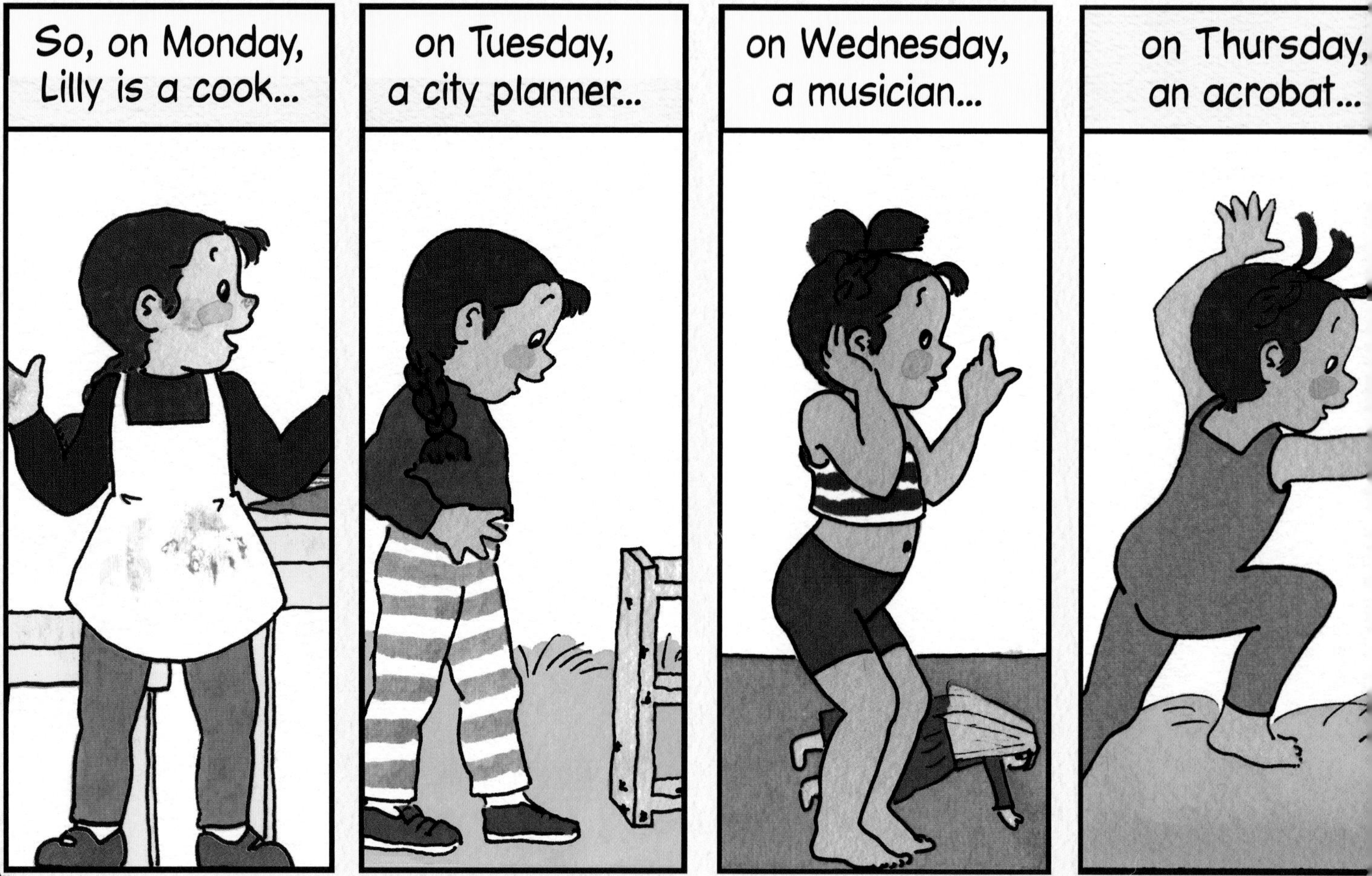
So, on Monday, Lilly is a cook...
on Tuesday, a city planner...
on Wednesday, a musician...
on Thursday, an acrobat...

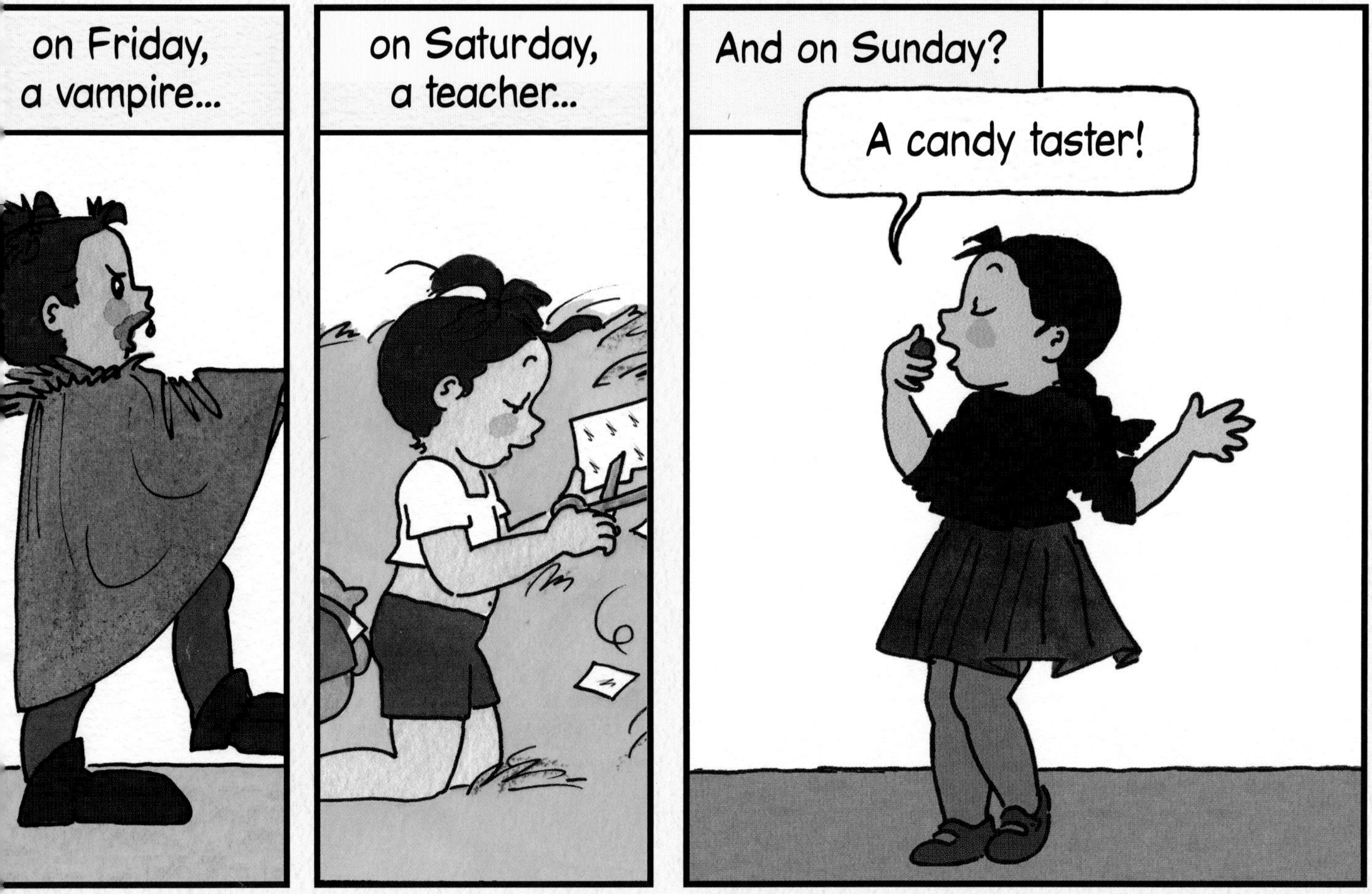
on Friday,
a vampire...
on Saturday,
a teacher...
And on Sunday?
A candy taster!

ABOUT THE AUTHOR

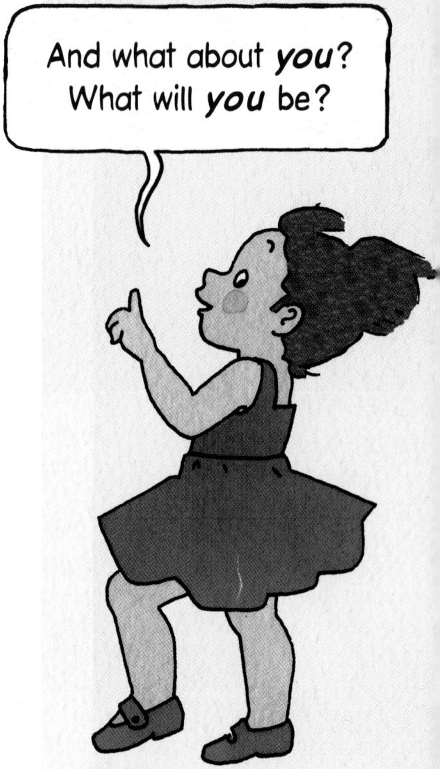
And what about *you*? What will *you* be?

Agnès Rosenstiehl is the beloved writer and artist of nearly a hundred children's books, many featuring the deceptively simple antics of "Mimi Cracra," Silly Lilly's French alter ego. About her first TOON Book, *Silly Lilly and the Four Seasons*, the well-known historian and critic Leonard Marcus said, in a starred review in *Publishers Weekly*: "[The] comic moments . . . that Rosenstiehl extracts from her rigorously pared-down materials draw us directly into Lilly's emotional world, where attention is routinely paid to everything, from a lowly dandelion on up. To know Lilly is to want to know what she has to say."

In 1995, Agnès Rosenstiehl received the prestigious Grand Prize for Children's Books from the Société des Gens de Lettres. Agnès is a scholar of literature as well as music, and is married to an eminent mathematician. She lives in a country house with a garden, hidden in the center of Paris. She has four children and fifteen grandchildren.

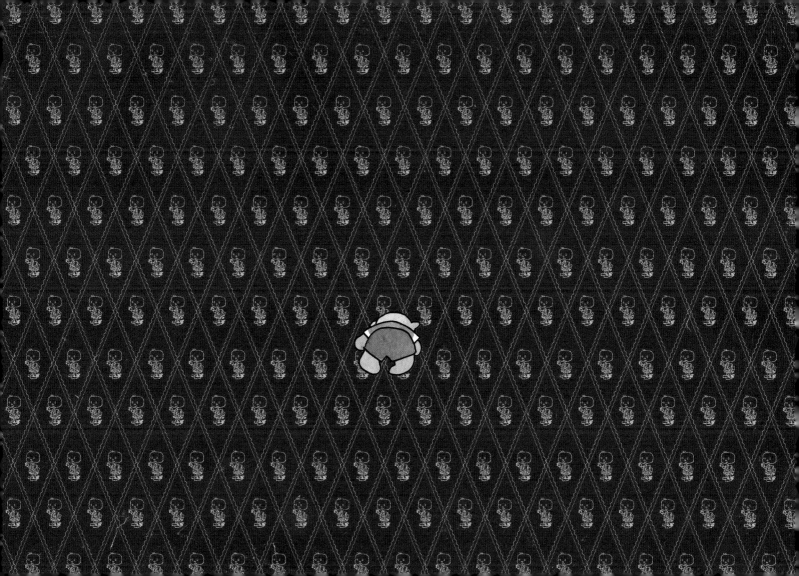

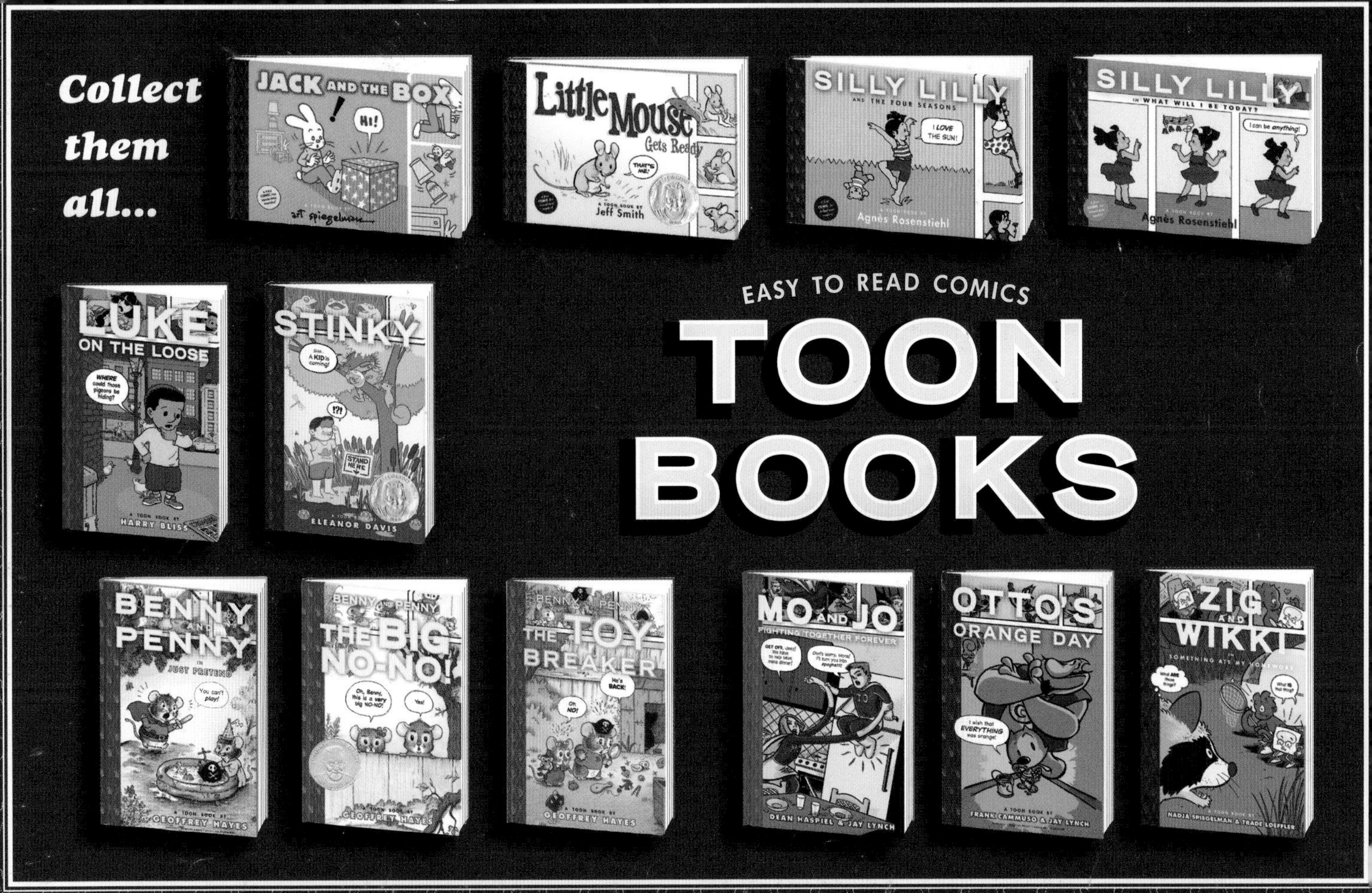
Collect them all...
JACK AND THE BOX
HI!
art spiegelman
Little Mouse Gets Ready
THAT'S ME!
A TOON BOOK BY Jeff Smith
SILLY LILLY AND THE FOUR SEASONS
I LOVE THE SUN!
A TOON BOOK BY Agnès Rosenstiehl
SILLY LILLY IN WHAT WILL I BE TODAY?
I can be anything!
A TOON BOOK BY Agnès Rosenstiehl
LUKE ON THE LOOSE
WHERE could those pigeons be hiding?
A TOON BOOK BY HARRY BLISS
STINKY
A KID is coming!
!?!
STAND HERE
ELEANOR DAVIS
EASY TO READ COMICS
TOON BOOKS
BENNY AND PENNY IN JUST PRETEND
You can't play!
A TOON BOOK BY GEOFFREY HAYES
BENNY AND PENNY IN THE BIG NO-NO!
Oh, Benny, this is a very big NO-NO!
Yes!
A TOON BOOK BY GEOFFREY HAYES
BENNY AND PENNY IN THE TOY BREAKER
He's BACK!
Oh NO!
A TOON BOOK BY GEOFFREY HAYES
MO AND JO FIGHTING TOGETHER FOREVER
DEAN HASPIEL & JAY LYNCH
OTTO'S ORANGE DAY
I wish that EVERYTHING was orange!
A TOON BOOK BY FRANK CAMMUSO & JAY LYNCH
ZIG AND WIKKI IN SOMETHING ATE MY HOMEWORK
A TOON BOOK BY NADJA SPIEGELMAN & TRADE LOEFFLER